A.K. KULSHRESHTH's short stories have been published in literary magazines and anthologies in eight countries. Together with his mother, he has translated four books from Hindi to English. In 2021, he completed *Bride of the City*, the first ever translation into English of the classic 1949 Hindi novel *Vaishali Ki Nagarvadhu*. His first novel *Lying Eyes* was longlisted for 2022 Epigram Books Fiction Prize.

A.K. KULSHRESHTH

LYING EYES

A Novel

BALESTIER PRESS
LONDON · SINGAPORE

Balestier Press
Centurion House, London TW18 4AX
www.balestier.com

Lying Eyes
Copyright © A.K. Kulshreshth, 2022

First published by Balestier Press in 2022

A CIP catalogue record for this book is available from the British Library.

ISBN 978 1 913891 37 4

Cover design by Zoya Chaudhary

LYING EYES

PART 1

1

Ah Ding Looks Into a Mirror

2005, Ah Ding

I WILL DIE SOON. Everybody dies. You will as well—don't get me wrong. It's nothing to do with me, of course. I'm not wishing it on you. When I get home and close the door, I get out of my wheelchair. Oh, that look. Don't give me that look. I have to live, for now, even if it's not for too long. The last five years, I've done this. Selling tissues. It's easier to sell if I am in a wheelchair. That's thinking from the customer's viewpoint, my last boss would have said. He was thirty years younger than me.

That's not the point. The point is, I get out of the wheelchair and stand in front of the mirror. Again. I didn't always do this. I only started after she spoke to me. I still stand straight. Almost. I look at myself. My skin with its splotches. One side of my face drooping. The hair almost gone. That big wart on the top of my left cheek, the big bulb of my nose. I think of her. She can't have long to live either. But she has longer than me. She has money. Her skin glows of it. And her eyes. They aren't clouded, like mine.

That must be why she recognized me first. I was in front of the escalator. It's the right place to be. I catch people's eyes just after they've finished stuffing themselves in the hawker centre. Bak kut teh, kueh, carrot cake, chicken rice, nasi lemak. You get it all.

Guaranteed, after a heavy meal, one in ten will stop for me. I get there early, at six. It's still dark, but people are trickling in.

They were coming down at seven in the morning. She and a young couple. Young, as in they could have been her son and his wife. This year, even before I met her and things got much worse, I've been dozing off in the mornings. Just another sign that I'm headed for the long sleep soon. I hope they find me before the maggots get to me.

Anyway, I had dozed off, and that thing happened again. You know, when your head rolls down too low, and your neck hurts. And then you wake up.

I woke up to find her looking at me. She looked without seeing me first. People often do. I looked straight into her eyes. It's much more effective than saying anything, especially with someone who has had a good meal. She was speaking. The man in front of her had his face turned up and backwards. The young woman was leaning forward, hanging on to every word.

I saw them frown as she stopped speaking. They followed her gaze. All three of them were looking at me. The escalator brought them down in a few seconds. The man slowed down as they neared me.

She kept walking. She wore a white top and a dark skirt. Her shoes were dark blue, with a shining white lining. The woman with her wore shorts. She had long, sleek legs and was taller by a head. Her hair was coloured light brown.

Their perfumes were different. One was strong, the other delicate. It was hard to say who wore which. They smelled of progress, happiness, health. She will die soon, the old woman, but she will not die alone. She did right back then.

*

She is back the next morning, alone. She stops in front of me. Her clothes are the same kind. The shoes too. Her perfume was the strong one.

"We met sixty years ago. I know you," she says. "I thought about you very often. I searched for you." She speaks Mandarin with the air of those who can also speak English.

"Eh?"

"We walked together to Bukit Panjang. In 1945."

It comes back to me, as clear as … as clear as anything can be.

"Three for one dollar," I say.

She stands there for a while. She takes the three packets I held out and puts two back. She fishes out a ten-dollar note from her shiny leather bag with two big letters on it. She puts the note on top of my box of tissues.

"I don't have change," I say.

"There's a reason why I'm giving you ten dollars," she says. "I saw you nodding your head and moving your hand in your sleep." She stretches the fingers of her right hand and swivels her palm. "It came back to me." She lowers her eyes and walks away.

Something about the way she says that reminds me of a long, sweaty day sixty years ago. From the steps at the market entrance, she looks over her shoulder. I turn my wheelchair to follow her. She is silhouetted against the bright light outside, her crisp white shirt standing out against the small shrine and the tree with its bright yellow flowers. Our eyes meet, and she smiles at me as if she is an aunt who has caught her nephew being naughty.

It is her, all right. Even with my failing eyes, it is clear as day. I last saw that face in a dim yellow light. For many years, I thought about her, wondered how she had made out in life. How many years? I do not know. Perhaps twenty or thirty, even as I tried to erase everything else that had happened around those years.

And in that moment when our eyes meet again, I remember how I had once longed to kiss her forehead. I remember the vibrations of the bus, the smoky smell of its charcoal engine.

I turn the wheelchair back towards the escalator to shut her out of my view. From somewhere in the folds of my memory, my teacher Mr Cheng's words come back to me: you can be cautious of the future, but not of the past.

Wrong again. That Mr Cheng—he was so wrong, so often. And with such confidence. I have to be cautious of my past still. I would like to believe that enough time has flowed, that the past is behind me. But that chance meeting with the woman proves again that it is not.

That day, I leave work early. In any case, I don't usually stay much beyond five in the evening. I cross over to take bus 123M for the ride home. The 5:20 bus driver knows about me because he's seen me fold the wheelchair and walk up the steps at Block 106 once when it looked like rain. He doesn't give me attitude.

I don't stay back at the market, and I don't waste time like the bunch of losers who hang out at the coffee shop in Block 107. I like to get home before seven. At seven, the lights in the corridor come on. The rows of gates remind me too much of prison in that light. At around six, the setting sun lights up the whole floor. My flat is on level nine. It's mine till I can pay the rent.

That day, the little girl from the Indian family is toddling around, dressed only in white underpants, her short curly hair falling over her face. She sees me coming and gives me a dimpled smile. She runs into her house. Their gate and door are open, as always, and an Indian film song with its thudding drumbeats and weirdly high-pitched female voice spreads to every corner of the floor. They do not play it too loud, and no one has complained about it yet.

About a month ago, I asked the little girl if she wanted my custard puff. She said, "How did you know that I am hungry?" Her white teeth shone against her dark face. A little while later, I heard a smack, and her wail, over their Bollywood music. I hoped she got to eat it. It would be a shame if her fat mother had gobbled it up. I got one for myself after many months. I regretted the offer as soon as I made it. That is life.

They are okay, on the whole, that family. At least they do not cook too much. Most likely, like the others, they live on Maggi and things like that. If I'd had to bear the smell of curry on top of listening to the husband thwacking his wife on the other side of my flat, that would have been too much. As it happens, the place is comfortable enough. Some people have it worse. I do not think I am going anywhere from here, except when I drop dead.

The woman whose name I do not know still reminds me of 1945, which sets off a film that moves backwards in time till 1942. When I get out of the wheelchair and go to the cracked mirror in the bathroom, I take a long and hard look at myself. I imagine a hood with slits for the eyes covering my face and tightening itself until the bit around my neck feels like a noose. I finger the wart on my cheek to bring myself back to the present. I think of how fine the woman dresses and looks, and how different from me she has turned out. I think of her knowing that I knew she had spotted me right. It is just that, for me, that past is something I had wiped clean so that I could live.

Now that past is back, suffocating me, making me feel breathless when I wheel myself up the ramp on my way, making me look at my sagging face as I stand here in front of the mirror. When I shaved by the light of the dim bulb this morning—essential in my line of work—my hands trembled. Maybe that happened because I woke up panting. I often used to forget my dreams, but the one that woke me today is not going away any time soon. It was only a half-dream, anyway, about a cigarette butt being stubbed out on a pale hand. The hand was mine, and as the dream returns to flicker in my mind I smell burning flesh, though I don't feel any pain there. The pain is in my head. There is a bump where I knocked it.

It took a lifetime to put the past behind me. I could be forgiven for thinking that I would glide into a peaceful death. But life brought her face-to-face with me and prodded her into remembering me. I maintain that I don't remember her.

That is all right. That is the only way it could be because, of course, we walked together. I was there, but I was then a different me. The walk—let's just say it never happened.

2

Have We Met Before?

1945, Ah Ding

"HAVE I SEEN YOU BEFORE?" Ah Ding asked. He expected her to be sarcastic, to mock him, to use one of the many tricks that pretty women knew. His words came out before he had time to think because it was true, perhaps, that he had seen her somewhere. Or at least someone like her. It might have been a different setting he had seen her in. A different light, perhaps. It may have been across the road, in the Da Yong Ya amusement park, in which case she may even have been a coffee girl. There was something about her face.

She faltered, and her eyes widened. First, it was fear he saw in her deep brown eyes. Now fear was something he knew all about. He had felt it often in the last three years. On rare occasions, he had inflicted it. He hated himself when he had done that, and that made him hate his victims even more. Those men—the two of them— might even be alive now. He hoped not.

From fear, he saw her expression turn to fury.

"No! That's a stupid question! And an old trick! Don't think I'll fall for it!" The childish tinge in her voice surprised him when she spoke like that. She was younger than she looked. It might have been the loose-fitting samsui woman's samfoo that she wore or the stiff way she walked, so unlike the hip-swinging gait one would expect from a young girl.

He peered at her. Her eyes were red and moist. She definitely wasn't pretending. Maybe she wasn't right in the head. There had only been the two of them walking in this direction, away from the city. They had waited for the STC bus for more than an hour. Opposite them, the amusement park showed no signs of life in the late morning. It would creak into action after noon. The mixed smells of teh and kopi wafted out from a shop right behind them, on Chun Tin Road.

He watched as she took in a deep breath and swayed as if those smells had got to her head. She looked vulnerable. And desirable. The thought had crossed his mind then for the first time. He had seen her somewhere. He hadn't made it up.

A river of people flowed towards the city. Many men were cycling all the way there. A few of them had children perched on the carriers fixed to the backs of their cycles. Once in a while, a trishaw would trundle by. They were a rare sight in that part of Singapore. Two buses had already driven by, their charcoal-fired engines wheezing with their unusually heavy loads. Both had cleared the waiting crowd at that junction of Upper Bukit Timah Road and Jalan Jurong Kechil. The crowd had built up again and was getting restless. The rush had begun early morning, as people flocked towards Municipal Building to watch the Japanese surrender.

It was just the two of them waiting to go the other way. Her hand strayed now and then to pat the side of her right thigh. It must be where she had her money, in the pocket of her trousers.

In front of the amusement park was a row of hoardings. "Drink More Beer!" exhorted one. Another showed a real tiger springing out of a Tiger Balm bottle. Like everything else, the hoardings had turned dusty and pale. Tatters of *The Synonan Shimbun* fluttered about in the late morning breeze.

She had avoided meeting his eyes since he had walked there. He had no wish to see the surrender, however much he had looked forward to it. It could be dangerous for him. After a few minutes, he squatted. He found standing still very tiring. She leaned against the pillar of a shophouse for a long time before giving in and squatting like him.

"Will there not be a bus today?" She spoke in a mumbling kind of way.

He could not quite figure what was unusual about her voice. Something about the way she had asked that question made him pity her. He knew she had been building up her courage to ask him. She had just blurted out the question without addressing him first.

"It looks like it," he said. "I'll wait awhile, then start walking. I'm going to Bukit Panjang. It should take an hour."

He turned to look back at her. She lowered her gaze and nodded.

He heard the distant rumble first. He sprang to his feet as it became louder. Then the front of the truck tipped over the line where Upper Bukit Timah Road met the clear blue sky. He cursed, and a sound from behind him made him look over his shoulder. The woman struggled to her feet. He saw the change in her face as she stopped craning to see what was coming their way.

It was a green Bedford truck, not a bus. As it loomed closer, the mass of its passengers morphed into a group of smartly dressed soldiers in fatigues and helmets. The muzzles of their rifles glinted. From the other side of the road, the throng broke into cheers. One of the children, a plump boy, even had a Union Jack and was waving it as he bumped up and down on the carrier of a cycle.

The soldiers waved back to the crowd. One of them, a tall gaunt blond man who wore his helmet at a jaunty angle, looked at him with a glitter in his eyes.

He looked at the white man, this smartly dressed conquering soldier who was so different from the ones who had been around in 1942. He spat. The truck was close enough now for him to feel its vibrations and to see the soldier's face tense up. Their eyes locked for a fraction of a second before the truck hurtled by.

There was a lump in his throat. He would walk, he decided. He turned to look at the woman. Her face had softened, as if she approved of what he had done.

"I will walk," he said.

"Yes," she said, and fell in step behind him. It was odd that they should be together and still be apart. He let it be.

They walked. The rush on the other side of the road was thinning out. On their side, it was only the two of them. It was like any other September day. The air was thick and humid. A film of sweat made his shirt stick to him. He had a thick wad of banana money in his right pocket and the ten-dollar note from 1942 in an envelope in his shirt pocket. That ten-dollar note had been his lucky charm. Back in 1942, he had considered throwing it away. He had held on to it without reason. The idea that the British would be back was laughable then.

This was 1945. They were back. His lips puckered, and a song came to them. He had already whispered a few bars before he knew it. It was a Li Xianling song, one of Colonel Oishi's favourites. He turned to the woman, afraid she might think he was getting fresh again. Not that there was anything wrong with that. Man and woman—together and alone—it was only natural for the thought to press in on him. She had a scent, and he had a smell, and they must mix in this humid air.

She had drawn closer. She was walking by his side now.

"I know that song," she said.

"Why don't you sing it? You have a nice voice. Really."

"Here? While walking?"

The look on her face made him feel lighter. She smiled like a girl should when she chides a boy she doesn't care for yet. There was no contempt.

Man and woman. This was life, and perhaps this year would be the start of a better life. And for him, if only he could forget Fusang, he would become a whole man again. He had been to whorehouses a few times before he realized he was being a fool. At the comfort station, where Oishi arranged tickets for him, he went until the end because it was free. It might have been because he did the woman some good, and he felt good about that. But honestly, he knew he was not a good man.

The shops on Chun Tin Road were busy. He had not wanted to walk by all those prying eyes. It was good to have the woman with him. Fewer people would recognize him. Perhaps. Anyway, he was not the only one who had worked for the Japs. There had been thousands. They could not single him out.

Across the road, Da Yong Ya, the entertainment complex with its hotchpotch of stalls, was sleepy. A few women had got into action, though, sweeping the street.

"You can never win there, you know," he said. "I learnt the hard way." He wanted to keep her talking so that they would look like a normal couple.

She frowned. She wanted to say something but didn't know what to say.

"Did you only go there to eat?" he asked.

"No," she said. She did not like the topic. "What do they have there?"

He could not help looking at her in that way, which brought a flush to her cheeks. "You mean you don't—did you not live here? Were you ... outside? In ...?"

She looked scared now. She tried to hold back a gulp travelling down her throat, but she could not.

How could she not know? Not that it mattered if she was going to be hard to get, anyway. But really, it was just his luck. Just when she had opened up to him—he knew she had—and he had got her smiling and talking, he had to ask her stuff that made her withdraw. But it wasn't anything strange he had asked. Ah, women.

A small stone had got caught in his sandal. "Can you wait a bit?"

he asked. At least that was easy to answer. She still had a sullen look. She nodded when she saw what he was doing. He tried to shake the stone out, but when that didn't work, he stood on one foot, took off his sandal and gave it a good shake. He swayed and almost fell before steadying himself. He probed around with a finger to make sure the sandal was smooth inside.

He had been a fit young man only three years ago. The training for Dalforce had been too little, too late. But he—and most of the others—had been strong, lean and full of energy. Now he had a belly. When he looked in the mirror—it was usually only in Oishi's office that he had access to one—he saw a pudgy, calculating man with tired eyes.

Was she silently mocking him? He peered at her. Her face was still taut, as if she was scared he would ask her more questions about where she had been in those three years, the Syonan years. He would get to the bottom of it, he would. But gently.

He mapped out the way to the village in his mind. They would cross the Nissan Factory, the Syonan Chureito Shrine, the Hume Factory, and then, it was just the road with rubber plantations and fields on either side, as far as he remembered, until the right turn for Bukit Panjang at the tenth mile.

His armpits and neck were drenched in sweat. He was quite thirsty, but he didn't want to go to the busy shops on their side of the road. They started walking again. She stayed a step behind him now. She was strange. He would let her be for some time.

The vibrations announced themselves long before the rhythmic hiss and rattle of the train deafened them. It chugged by at a leisurely pace. He wished there was a way he could jump on it and leap off near the village.

"If only we could get on that train," she said.

He turned to her, and she shrugged as if to apologize for a silly thought.

"That's exactly what I was thinking," he said.

She caught up with him again.

"It's been so long since … since I saw one. I mean, it's been more than a month since the last train," she said.

He knew right away that she had said that to show she had been somewhere close by. How could she have seen the trains but not known about Da Yong Ya?

"Where is it going, do you think?" she asked.

"I guess taking soldiers towards Woodland or Kranji, or somewhere," he said.

"It would get us to Bukit Panjang in minutes, no?" She smiled. Her teeth were spotted but healthy and white. From a deep recess in his mind, he remembered a Kempeitai man telling him that the way to judge a woman's ability to serve for a long time was to check her teeth. Same as you would check a cow back in his village. He pushed the thought away.

"What?" she asked.

"Nothing," he said.

"But I thought you said—"

"Nothing. I was just thinking about how long it will take. We've just got started."

"I will walk faster," she said.

*

Sweat made his shirt cling to his body. At least they were walking fast, and she kept up with him without complaining. Fusang would have smacked him and said something funny to slow him down. Something like, who are you running to meet, your mother? The thought came to him without warning. He shivered. Was it this woman who had ferreted out the long-suppressed memory of his love? Or was it Fusang's spirit that made him think of the woman in that way?

"What are you thinking?" she asked. She was curious, that

woman. Sometimes warm, sometimes cold. And it was true, he did have the sense he had seen her before. He wasn't making it up when he had asked. He wasn't stupid to try a trick like that.

He looked at her and shook his head.

"Isn't it about your wife?" she asked.

She smiled when he gaped at her. Her smile had a constrained quality. It reminded him of Oishi and some of the other Japs, in a way. Like them, she smiled, but her smile did not light up her eyes. Yet there was a difference. She felt fear inside, whereas Oishi and his men inflicted fear.

They had reached hill 345. The straight road on their left and the steps up to the top of the hill and the Syonan Chureito Shrine, in their perfect geometry, bathed in the bright light of the day. The table-shaped top of the mountain stood out against a clear blue sky splattered with a few straggling clouds.

She bumped into him. It was the first time he got close enough to get a whiff of the scent of her body. In that moment, he thought how strange it was that the sweaty flesh of a young woman should arouse a man so.

"What?" she said.

"The shrine. The tower!" he said. "It's gone already!"

She gulped. As clear as reading a book, he sensed her irritation giving way to fear of admitting she did not know what he was talking about. There must be a story here. Perhaps he would find it out, perhaps not.

"You know, they built a shrine here, at the top of the hill. The Japs. From here, you could see the pillar rising high, very high. And there was a small cross behind it, for the British also. And now ... it's gone! Just like that."

She turned up at the straight, ascending road and then turned back towards him, her brows knit in concentration. She must be curious about all this. All women were curious, anyway. She would want to know about it without talking about why she did not know what had happened in these last three years.

"I think I know what it means, Chureito," she said. "It means a pillar."

He had not expected that. "Ah, I never thought about it," he said. "But it makes sense because that's what it was." He chose his words carefully now to tell her about it without rubbing it in that he knew she had never seen it. "It was high, very high. Taller than a two-storey building, even. And yes, I saw it only a few days ago. That's why I was shocked."

Her eyes became moist. He looked pointedly at the barren hilltop to give her time to wipe them with her sleeves. He stood looking for a while, hands on his hips. Then, without turning to her, he said, "Who could have thought all this … Anyway, let's go, shall we?"

She replied with a syllable, and they started walking. She walked half a step behind him. He did not try to talk to her. In the short time that they had been together, she had swung through many moods. She was a strange one, even for a woman.

He was a bit lost in thought, and it took him a while to register that she had spoken. He put the words together with a delay. "I'm going home," she had said. "I do not know …" she had trailed off.

"Where is home?" he asked.

"I told you, Bukit Panjang."

"But where there?"

"Near the wet market."

"I know that place. My teacher used to live there."

"Mr Cheng?"

"Yes! Do you know him?"

"Not well. But yes, we know him … everyone knows him. And his wife is a nice woman."

He gulped. That night in Bukit Timah, when the Chengs had died but insisted that he should live … He felt faint. It must be the thirst. Maybe he should have had a drink on Chun Tin Road, after all. There was a nice sarabat tea stall there.

"She died," he said.

"Who?"

"The wife. And Mr Cheng as well."

The woman was quiet. He wanted to stop and tell her to come out with it. He imagined grabbing her shoulders and shaking them. But he thought of her eyes watering, and his anger left him.

"It has been a horrible time," she said.

The top of the Nissan Factory came into view. "I am sure this will become Ford Factory again," he said.

He looked at her from the corner of his eye. He had wanted to break it to her gently. Her face was tense again. Then, to his surprise, a hint of a smile lit it up. Her gaze was drawn to a spot, quietly pulled away, but it returned there. He followed her gaze.

It was a hawker, an Indian, with a mobile drink stall. He stood at the side of the road, just in front of the factory. Two rows of empty bottles of RC Cola and Peacock tonic water glinted in the bright light of the day.

When he looked at her, she was grinning back. She was unguarded, like a thrilled child.

"We got lucky," he said.

The hawker was an old man in a white shirt. As they approached him, he followed their progress with a smile. When they were close, he broke into a broad grin.

"How come you are on the wrong side of the road, Abang?" He spoke Malay.

"I could ask you the same," Ah Ding replied with a laugh.

"Ah, I usually come here because of the factory workers. It seems they are closed for a long time. I was about to cross over."

"I'll have …" Ah Ding found it hard to make up his mind. The cola would be costly, but it would feel heavenly. He could already imagine its tingling cold coursing through his overheated body. And he did want to impress her. He couldn't ask the Mamak how much, though.

The old man's teeth had many gaps. His grin had broadened. He had seen life, this man. "It's the usual," he said. "50 cents for the RC cola, 20 for the Peacock."

"I feel like an RC," Ah Ding said to the woman. "You?"

She said, "It's costly ..."

The Mamak looked at her with interest. He must be pondering that she was obviously not the wife, Ah Ding thought. The wife would have decided for both.

"It's a long walk," Ah Ding said. He turned to the hawker and said, "Two RCs." He fumbled in his back pocket and got a two-dollar banana note out of a neatly folded pack of notes.

The hawker handed him back the change, pausing for a moment to calculate. Ah Ding looked at the dollar he had got back and considered telling the man to keep it. It would soon become useless, he was sure. But he had seen the Mamak look in the same way when he had received the note. There was no point thinking too much about these things.

The Mamak's movements were slow. He opened the icebox and took out two bottles. As he popped them open, barely perceptible fumes floated upwards from them. The sound and the sight had a cooling effect.

The woman thanked Ah Ding and looked into his eyes when he gave her the bottle. Their fingers did not brush. He held his bottle against his cheek first before taking one big gulp. He closed his eyes to savour the moment.

When he opened them, the woman was looking at him. She turned her eyes away at once. With her eyes lowered, she puckered her lips and raised the bottle to them. Her lips closed around the mouth of the bottle and stayed there for what seemed like a long time. Ah Ding felt a stirring of desire. He turned his gaze away just in time to avoid her flashing eyes as they turned to rebuke him.

He swished the cola in his mouth and swallowed it as slowly as he could. Every drop must count. He kept his eyes away from her, but the image of her lips closing on the rim of the bottle just would not go away.

He fought off a belch with all his might. It was a losing battle. When it came, the belch was soft but unmistakable. And she belched at the same time. He could not help looking her way. Their eyes met. She started laughing before he did.

"It's been many, many years since I had one," she said. "Maybe five years? I remember it was my ... birthday." For the first time, her smile spread to her eyes.

"I've had a few," he said. "It's nice on a day like this."

On the other side of the road, a bus trundled into view and came to a stop. No one got out. The conductor cried out to the passengers to move in and not be shy. When it lurched forward and left, its engine screeching in protest, the waiting crowd at the stop had cleared.

"So, not going to watch the surrender?" the Mamak asked.

Ah Ding shrugged. He did not want to talk about it. "Did you see any buses go this way?" he asked.

"Only one when I had just got here. Not in the last two hours," the old man said. "It looks like they are only running the other way today."

Ah Ding nodded and turned away, glad that he had changed the topic. He wanted to talk to her now, while the warmth induced by the cold drink lasted, but he couldn't do it with the Mamak there. And he did want to make the drink last.

She was taking small gulps as well. She lowered her eyes modestly when her lips sucked on the mouth of the bottle, as if not looking up made her invisible. She held the drink in her mouth for a long time before her throat made a delicate swallowing motion. She belched again, and her eyes twinkled.

They were standing in the shade of a large tree. Something small, perhaps a bud, fell on her, and she brushed it away with a graceful wave of her hand.

A hollow sound came from his bottle. It was empty. He tilted it up all the way up and got a last drop out of it. He waited for her to finish. She made hers last much longer. Before they had stopped, the air seemed to singe his nostrils. He felt much better now. She handed him her bottle when she had finished. He was careful not to touch her fingers. She blushed for a fleeting instant as she thanked him. Then her mask came on.

He put the bottles on the trolley, gave the Mamak a quick wave to pre-empt any more talk, and they started off again. The RC Cola had talked for him. He was lucky.

3

Are You Not Going Home?

1945, Ah Ding

SHE WAS BY HIS SIDE AGAIN. The tiredness in his feet and back had evaporated. A bright yellow bird flitted between a pair of trees on their side of the road. The woman and Ah Ding turned to each other as if to say, "Did you see that?" They smiled and walked on.

He played the image of her lips parting and closing in on the rim of the RC Cola bottle again. It became a cinema, and her samsui woman's dress became a cheongsam. Her lips were thicker and redder, even in that black-and-white montage. He imagined himself slipping out of his body and following her as she walked by his side. Her dowdy, shapeless dress and the stiffness of her gait did not completely suppress the swaying of her wide hips.

Did she know he was stripping her in his mind? Holding her shoulders and bending over to kiss the nape of her sweaty neck, to run his tongue in a small circle on her puckering skin, to taste her saltiness?

All his time during the occupation, he had seen men and women getting on with their lives as much as they could. Marrying, having children, cremating the dead—except the ones who disappeared, of course. He had stayed broken, knowing no love, making pointless visits to whores for a while, and then settling for those times at the comfort station that Oishi had arranged for him.

Now with this woman, it was different, perhaps. The scent of her worked in the same animal way, but there was more to it than that. There must be a reason why they both were here, and no one else was. There was the puzzle of where she had been and what she had been up to. Whatever it was, it was forgivable. If she told him the truth. Her smile, which tinged her cheeks but did not light her eyes, would look so much better if it was not strangled. He imagined her lying trembling below him, slick with sweat, her heart still thudding, her eyes moist and smiling.

She let out a gasp, something that sounded like "Ai-ee," she said, "don't you hear that?"

He had heard it so often that it had not registered. It was the barking of a pack of dogs. A long time ago, Cheng had told them about Li Bai's poem, *Thoughts in Night Quiet*, and Ah Ding had cracked a joke about his last night having been remarkable only for the barking of dogs. Cheng had been forgiving, as usual.

Now, as the barking grew louder, a stray dog came scurrying out of the undergrowth by the roadside. A few seconds later, a big group of dogs burst out of a thicket and into view. They were a good distance away, but their barks were ferocious enough to make him baulk for a moment.

She stopped. "Shall we go back?" she asked. Her eyes were wide and her face pale. Her breath was shallow. Ah, fear. He had seen so much of it, and each time he thought he had seen it all. This was nothing.

He shrugged and made a flicking motion with his hand. "Don't worry about it," he said. "They were chasing that one away." He pointed to the lone dog that was running away. "They won't attack us. Not here and not in broad daylight."

Just as he said it, the dogs ratcheted up their barking a level higher and ran closer to them. Their quarry, a feeble black dog with droopy, watery eyes, looked over its shoulder. It lowered its head and scampered faster. Its tormentors were a few hundred feet away, and they slowed down as the pariah sped up.

A frisson of fear made him shudder when the dogs came running towards them. He looked around. They were quite alone on that stretch of road. To their left, less than half a mile away, would be the Hume Pipes factory, on top of a steep embankment. It was surely closed.

He looked for something resembling a stick. There was nothing in sight. A distant hum sounded from the far end of the road. It grew into a powerful roar. A shiny military truck lumbered into view. Its noise was impossibly loud. As it grew closer, he saw that there were two more behind it. They were hurtling down the road at a speed he had not seen in a long time. They must be powered by diesel, not charcoal. As they whizzed by, sucking in the air around them, they blasted him and the woman with their smoky exhaust. They carried dark-skinned Indian troops.

The dogs scurried away without a whimper.

This was life, was it not? Man, woman. Man, animal. His euphoria had vanished with that prick of fear. It made no sense, but he still felt a thudding in his ribcage. Had she noticed? She looked away when he turned towards her.

They walked on in silence.

*

On a moonlit night a week ago, the Japs had initiated the process of withdrawing into their shell. The rumours had floated around for months before thickening and descending on the city, smothering it into a stunned silence. What did it mean, this new chapter in a book that he had never asked to be part of?

It meant Ah Ding stood in the dark, frozen, looking at the reflection of the bright moon that had just a sliver loped off, thinking how much better the river looked at night. Thinking it was ridiculous to be there, scared enough to fear wetting his pants, and thinking of the moon and the water.

Knowing it could have been him instead of the other man, Yan Hong. Only minutes had separated their fates. He had watched as Yan Hong made a run for it, in his clumsy, shuffling way, and then came up short as if someone had pulled him from behind, by his collar.

There was no one behind. A man in a white shirt had stepped out of the shadows, right in front of Yan Hong. The man walked with a limp. His spectacles glittered. Ah Ding could almost see the creases on the man's forehead as the man half-smiled.

"So, running dog," the man had said. There was no malice in his tone. "We meet again."

Yan Hong went down on his knees. There was nothing else for him to do. There were four of them.

Not a word was spoken. The men who surrounded Yan Hong passed a long knife among themselves, each of them inflicting a cut.

Ah Ding felt the bile rising from his gut. He prayed it would not make him cough. He tried slowing his breath, but that only seemed to make it faster. The stench of the river filled his nostrils.

The men continued at it for a long time, even after Yan Hong stopped twitching. It was a quiet night. Above him, there were clothes out to dry. They fluttered in the cool breeze.

They would have cut Tiong up slowly, prolonging their pleasure—not unlike a pack of dogs—if he had not been hidden. He could have chosen his other shirt, the white one, instead of the dark-brown one he was wearing. That would have meant death.

The men left in different directions. The spectacled one gave them a perfunctory wave as if to acknowledge a routine job done reasonably well.

"Oh yes, it is the end," Oichi had told Ah Ding. "Many of us will slit our bellies. I would do it, but I still have much to contribute to this world. Now you, my friend …" He let out a tick, straight beam of smoke that diffused into a blue cloud. "You." He frowned. "You better get the hell out of here, out of the city. Do something to make yourself less recognizable."

He thought of the group of men who had chased Yan Hong, surrounded him and calmly slashed him to death. They would be MPAJA men, and there were hundreds more where they had come from. Could he escape? Where to? Malaya was not safe. Perhaps Sumatra? How could he do it with a bundle of banana money?

His meeting was over, and so was his relationship with Oishi. Ah Ding sat in silence for a long time before this sank in. When he got up, he still bowed low.

*

They were walking along Hume Pipes now. There was not a spot of shade. The sunburn on his right was hurting. Up ahead, the road shimmered in the heat. At the horizon, it seemed to melt into a pond. The bitumen felt soft. It exuded a hot vapour with a burnt smell. The stickiness of the heat strangled him.

She was walking in step with him. Was she humming to herself? That was what it sounded like. Her head swayed in time to the music in her mind.

Then, in a blip, she became pensive, almost as if something she had forgotten had returned to trouble her. She was mysterious, this woman.

"So you're a running dog?" she said.

He stopped short. "What?"

She was ahead of him now. She had to crane her neck to look at him. Her eyes were narrow and screwed up. Then her mask came on.

"Why are you shouting?" she said.

"What did you say?"

"Stop shouting first." She was breathing hard, and her voice quivered as if she was about to cry.

"I am not …" He realized his heart was thudding, and there was a hum in his ears. There was something wrong. The ground swayed. Dear God, he thought, not now. There was no one in sight to help if he fainted.

"I think I am not well."

She peered at him.

"You are not. I think you are not sane."

He lowered his head.

She crossed her arms and sighed. "I did not mean that. But …"

"No, it is true. I am not … I am not well. But don't … Let's just go."

He started walking.

She did not move. "What did you think I had said?"

He stopped. She must stay with him till Bukit Panjang. It was safer that way. Even if people looked for him, they would not look for a moustached man with a woman beside him.

"What?" she insisted.

"I thought you called me a running dog." He shrugged and motioned with his hand as he started walking again. This time she walked with him.

She frowned. "Why would I call you a dog?"

"I thought you said it."

"You are …" She stopped. She probably had the word insane in mind. "It must be the heat." She shrugged.

A trickle of sweat ran down the crown of his head to the back of his neck. "They call collaborators running dogs. Collaborators with the Japs."

She stopped. "You are one of them," she said. There was no expression in her voice. She spat, keeping her eyes locked on his.

The small gob of spit lay on the tar, a few inches from his feet.

His throat was dry when he gulped. He fought back another gulp but gave in to it. It hurt even more.

She was trembling. Her face was tight, as if she had clenched her jaws. Then, all of a sudden, she slumped and lowered her head.

"Let's keep walking," she said.

He started, and she fell in step behind him. The flapping of her slippers was the only sign that she was behind him.

The chugging sound must have been in the background for a while, but he did not notice it until it was too late. Two honks of a horn jolted him. By the time he looked over his shoulder, the snout of the green bus was already past them, and in a moment, it was receding into the distance, leaving its sputtering charcoal engine noise in its wake.

He stopped and raised his head skyward. If only they had heard it coming and waved it to a stop, they would have been getting their tickets punched now. But this was life. He was running from the past, and he was already so tired that the past could overtake him any time, without warning.

"It's all right," she said. "Isn't that Bukit Panjang Circus? After the slope?"

It was true. He had walked in a daze. Bukit Panjang Circus was less than half a mile away now. He nodded without looking back at her.

"Which part are you going to?" she asked.

He stopped and whirled around. "Why do you want to know?"

Her jaw fell. "I don't want to know. Let's keep going."

"No, why did you ask?" he said.

"I just asked. What can I do with what you tell me?" She was much softer now.

"Then why ask?"

She tilted her head to one side. Her thin eyebrows were knit, and her lips pressed. At that moment, he knew where he had seen her. It was how she had reacted those times as well.

"You are not right," she said. "Not right in the head." She made the sign with a revolving finger near her temple.

He wanted to say that he knew, but he choked on the words. A place to sit would be heavenly. His calves and the backs of his knees were aching.

"Did you know you were shouting? You were so loud—you were spitting! Your eyes looked like they would burst out," she said.

He shook his head.

"I thought not," she said. "There is nothing I can do, even if you tell me where you are going. I would not know whom to tell it to." She whispered now. "Let's go. It is not far." She started walking, and he joined her.

That was when it came to him where he had seen her. He had never seen her dressed properly, never outside in bright light. That was his excuse. What was hers? Was it that all men had become faceless to her?

She was frowning. Her forehead was lined. She caught him looking at her, and she looked away.

"I'm going home … after three years," she said. "They will be happy to see me." She could have been trying to convince herself.

"I have to meet someone at a coffee shop in the market," he said. "They will hide me for some time, till …"

"You didn't have to tell me that."

"I think I can tell you", he said.

She stopped and turned to face him. "What do you mean?"

"I trust you," he said. He moved his head in an arc to signal that she should keep moving.

She did. The lines on her face softened.

"It did not take that long. It's not far now," he said.

She did not reply. Was she angry again? She was strange, but now that he had placed her, he felt different about her. He looked at her. She was lost in thought.

The stretch to Bukit Panjang Circus went by in a whirr. On a normal day, they would have had to look right and left, stop many times, wave their hands to make their way through the throngs of cyclists, cycle rickshaws and a few cars and buses. Today the place lay desolate. A Union Jack drooped on the flagpole in front of Bukit Panjang Police Station, across the crossing. There was a row of cars in front of the building, but no other signs of life.

"Shall we walk on the other side?" she asked. There were shophouses there, and they could use the five-foot way. With the slant of the sun, they would not really be in the shade, but there were trees along the road, and it would be a more pleasant walk.

The row of shops stretched for a few hundred feet. The five-foot way, a path formed by the covered fronts of the shops, was besieged by pieces of furniture and materials, but the passage remained clear for passers-by to walk through unhindered. At intervals, trees and bamboo mats screened out some of the scorching heat.

The shops were all closed—except for the Soon Li coffee shop. That was the one place he had feared crossing. It was strange that it had come to this. He had spent many hours of his life there, with his friends. Their decision to join the Dalforce was taken over steaming kopi at Soon Li. He used to inhale the vapour rising from the thick black broth—he preferred black because it was a bit cheaper, to be honest—with his eyes closed, before taking his first sip. He remembered opening his eyes to find Chiang looking at him, Yeow rolling his eyes. The discussion turned to the rumours of the Japanese landings in Malaya and Siam. All that felt as if it had happened just yesterday. The days went slowly, the years went fast.

And here he was, walking with her past Soon Li. She had slowed down as well and lowered her head like him, as if doing that was protection from being recognized.

He must talk to keep up the pretence of them being a couple. "Did you not want to buy something? For home?"

"Buy?" she said, startled. She looked at him and then looked away slowly. "I have no … I do not know yet. I will go there first. I will see how they are. I mean, I have not …"

He could have completed her lines for her. His heart ached for her, and he wished he could squeeze her arm and tell her it would be fine.

The touch of the coarse cotton on his palms alerted him to the fact that he had followed his mind. She stopped and swivelled to face him. An angry light flickered and died out in her eyes. Her lips parted, but they closed before she said anything.

He pulled his hand back, and his head fell. His shame must have shown. She sighed and looked away. "Let's keep going."

He led the way. He was glad to move on. There were eyes on them, and he felt the weight of the stares on his back.

A rhythmic creak drew near. He looked over his shoulder. It was a cycle rickshaw. The driver wore a shirt caked in dirt and a Western hat with a wide brim. The mix was quite incongruous. It was tempting to call out to the man. It would be so much easier to be driven down this last stretch of road, past the lake on the left and on to the market. He imagined the breeze ruffling his sweaty head, her arm and thigh brushing his, the tension in their muscles as they strained to avoid leaning on each other.

It would not do. He could not make himself that visible.

"You may as well save the money," she said. "It is not too far, anyway."

She was full of surprises, this woman. He felt a surge of pity for her now, much after he had placed her in the comfort station at Jalan Jurong Kechil. He also knew that pity was the last thing she wanted. Perhaps all she wanted was to be home and not come out for a long time, except when there were no eyes on her. Perhaps. There were many of them, men and women, who were alive, and needed to know how to get on with what was left of life.

They were well out of sight of the men in the coffee shop now. That was a relief. Before the Synonan days, its smell of buttered coffee and cigarette smoke had intoxicated him as much as the talk. He felt a buzz when Cheng talked to the group, but looked at him more often than he looked at the others. The comfortable, cool touch of the marble tabletop on the skin of his arm during a hot afternoon, the stools worn into two smooth concave hollows by the butts of the mostly male visitors—was it really that long since he had felt those things?

Now, there was no butter and not that much coffee. Like the other coffee shops—the few that remained—Soon Li had become a seller of provisions and still offered a weak coffee without milk and sugar. The birdcages in its corners were missing, and the men who sat there maintained a silence that Ah Ding found oppressive. As the five-foot way ended, they were back in the sun, but soon the trees along the lake would give them respite.

"Are you all right now?" she asked.

"What do you mean?"

"You were ... I thought you were scared for a while."

She looked straight ahead. A line of sweat had formed on her temple. She brushed it aside with the back of her palm before it trickled into her eyes.

"I was," he said. "I still am. There were too many men in that coffee shop."

She nodded.

A raucous medley of bird cries sounded from a group of trees on their left. The pond came into sight. Its surface was dark green and still. In the distance, its far shore was cluttered with water hyacinths and weeds. Was he imagining it, or had the air turned a bit cooler? They slowed down.

He had not been here for many months now. It was more practical to share a room on Amoy Street since he had to report both to the Kempeitai office and the Police Headquarters. The few trips he made to see his parents left him unsettled and uncertain. Would they all have been better off if he had just kept his head down and not marched off into the war? His father had never once said, "I told you so." But the reproach lurked behind those dull eyes.

The surface of the lake looked perfectly placid if you did not pay attention. When you did, it melted into a quivering, lively membrane. He wanted to sit down here before getting to the rendezvous at the market. What if Oishi had not made the arrangements right? The images of the communists calmly slashing their quarry to death flickered in his mind's eye.

She was sobbing. He did not know when it had started. One moment, she had been by his side, just a few inches away from him, looking wistfully at the lake. The next moment, she slumped, and her shoulders heaved. She cried without a sound at first. Then a first sob sounded, and the sobs grew louder before receding into silence, even as her shoulders jerked, and the tears streamed down the edges of her hands, which she pressed into her face as if doing that would make her invisible.

He looked over his shoulder on both sides. There were a few people on the far side of the road, and some of them were crossing over to the shophouses. The rest were streaming towards Bukit Panjang Circus. There was no one in earshot.

He reached out to pat her shoulder. With a guttural cry, she pushed his hand away. She wiped her tears into the right sleeve of her dark dress. The shaking of her shoulders became less violent, her breath less raspy.

There was a thick log next to the shore. He pointed to it, and they walked over and sat on it. The worn wood was hard and uncomfortable on his buttocks, but his legs welcomed the lifting of their burden.

She buried her face in her hands again, but this time she did not cry. She sat still, now breathing in a deep, composed pattern. She let her hands fall by her sides and straightened her shoulders. Her eyes were dry and red and did not meet his. He let her be.

A few feet into the water, a splash set off ripples as a big fish surfaced and dived back. The ripples spread into the expanse of the lake before fading away.

"Are you all right now?" he asked.

She sighed. "I am afraid." Her voice was strained. She cleared her throat.

"Are you not going home?"

"I am. I do not know what will happen."

"I see."

"No, I don't think you know."

"Oh, I know." He spoke softly now. "They may not take you in?" Her eyes were more brown than black, he realized. They reflected a blurred mishmash of sun rays and foliage. She lowered her head, and the trance broke. "We should go now," he said. "I should be getting to the market."

4

Why Don't You Bless Me Instead?

1945, Ah Ding

HER SHOULDERS convulsed one last time, but she was steady when she looked at him. "You should not be late," she said. "Do you want to go? I am a bit tired. I can go later."

The hum of the cicadas turned a tone shriller. Ah Ding focused on it for a while. He sighed and said, "No, what's the point of being with you all this way if I go on my own now?"

Her brow crinkled before smoothening. She chuckled. "You need me to be with you? If they are looking for you, they won't be looking for a couple? Is that it?"

He shrugged.

"I'll take a minute more," she said. "Less. Is my face bad?"

It was, he told her, and she nodded.

"Do you need more time?" he asked.

"Yes, just a minute," she said.

She winced as she stood up. She stomped her foot a bit and walked stiffly to the shore. She knelt, lowered her head, cupped the water and sank her face into it. A dragonfly that was buzzing above the water gave way to her, spreading tiny whorls on the surface of the pond.

He sat on his haunches. When she mumbled something to herself and suddenly turned around, their eyes met for an infinitesimal moment before he lowered his gaze. She gave no indication that she knew he had been tracing the lines of her body in his mind.

"Shall we go?" she said.

"Will you be alright?"

"I do not know. I am not sure waiting here will be any use."

"Then we should go now," he said.

"Yes," she said. "Do you want to know more about me?"

The question surprised him. It struck him that she did not really understand. She had not recognized him as the man who came in and sat in silence because he could not do it.

"No," he said. "It's fine this way. In any case, I really don't want to tell you more about myself."

A smile flitted over her face. Her cheeks were still a bit puffed. "What did you do that there are men looking for you now?"

She flinched as he swivelled towards her. "No, I should not ask," she said. They kept walking.

"You can ask," he said, surprising himself. This time, her wan smile lingered. "You can't rule a city without the people of the city helping you. Now that help—it's up to you how to ask men for help. You can do it in a way that makes men say yes to you. There were thousands of us. I was one of many."

"I can believe that", she said.

There was a slight bend in the road, and the market with its two gables was visible already. The road, Jalan Cheng Hwa, buckled upwards steeply and was lined with shops on both sides. Most of them had cane mats half unrolled to keep out the sun.

A group of three boys came hurtling down the road, their voices rising to girlish pitch in their excitement. "My turn!" shouted one, but he was not fast enough to catch up with the leader, who held a stick to a whirring cycle tyre rim that slid on the road. The boy who lagged behind the other two ran with his head swaying wildly. He was jumping high into the air with each stride. The fluidity of their movements made Ah Ding feel lighter.

"Shall we cross over?" he asked. She nodded, and they walked to the other side.

"Did you do that when you were small?" she said.

It took him some time to realize that she had spoken, and then he had to parse back what his ears had heard, but his mind had not yet processed. "Yes," he said.

He felt her quizzical eyes on him as he scanned the row of shops and the entrance to the market. He had been told to look for a bicycle chained to the pipe that ran down the pillar at the eating house on the left of the market entrance. His contact would be a man who would spend a couple of hours in the eating house, with a rolled copy of *The Synonan Times* on his table. Would it still be published today, though?

It did not matter. There was no bicycle.

He slowed down and scanned the market entrance. The two vegetable shops in front were quiet as usual. The one on the left was run by a dour couple who kept their prices low. The one on the right had two boisterous brothers. Before the war, they used to be full of jostling shoppers of all ages and races. In the Syonan years, the meaning of vegetables had altered significantly. The default choice was tapioca, and sweet potatoes were luxuries.

If it had not been for the woman, he would have been caught as he reflected on this state of affairs. As it was, his being with her made him invisible to the men who were waiting for him. That was what he had counted on, and for once, fate had sided with him. To be fair, these last few days, it had smiled on him more than ever.

Between the two vegetable shops, a man stood with his hands in his pockets, a cigarette dangling from the corner of his mouth. His bespectacled eyes roved the street. Ah Ding was not good at remembering faces, but this one posed no problem for him. It was the MPAJA man who had led the trio that had cut Yan Hong to pieces.

Her fingers were surprisingly strong on his arm. Her grip almost hurt him.

"Do you need to sit?" She was peering at him, frowning.

He shook his head. "Keep talking to me. Is anyone looking this way?"

"No, I don't think so. Did you just see someone you need to hide from?"

"Yes. They will kill me if they see me."

She gulped. "What do you want to do?"

"Let's do what we've been doing. Walk."

"You looked like you were about to fall," she said.

"I am fine now," he said. "Let's walk towards your place."

"It's the village after the Malay kampung," she said. "You don't have to come there."

"I know. I can't stay here, and I don't have another place I would like to go to."

A group of three men, most likely coolies in the market, walked past them on the road. One of them smelled of a cigarette. Ah Ding's throat was dry in a way that made him crave the feeling of smoke caressing the back of his mouth. That was strange. It had been many years since he had felt this way. He had stopped smoking after Oishi stubbed out a cigarette on a prisoner. Ah Ding could not avert his eyes in time.

She was looking at him. She spoke with the exaggerated patience of someone who was repeating herself. "Shall we go on?"

"Yes," he said. He laughed but stopped short.

"What was that?" she said.

"I was pretending to laugh," he said.

"Don't try it again. You look scared enough to wet your pants." He nodded.

"And don't walk so fast, even if you want to scramble out of here. You will draw attention to yourself, and I can't keep up with you." She panted a bit.

He nodded. She was right. This stretch of Jalan Cheng Hwa was bustling with people. The crowd was oppressive, and he could not get out of there fast enough. But he must slow down. His shirt clung to his back and chest. It was a while since he had noticed the heat. Now his sweat had broken out in profuse abandon. Her face glistened as well, and her eyes had not lost their mistiness since she had cried.

They walked in silence. The din of the market faded away. There were rubber trees on the sides of the road now. The trees did not protect them from the afternoon sun, but there was just a hint of a breeze filtered by the shady plantation. The hum of the insects was the only sound for a long stretch, till the Malay kampung came into view, with its attap huts on stilts.

A baby's wail pierced the stillness, and an elder's scolding followed. It sounded like an old man scolding the mother because his afternoon nap had been disturbed.

Somewhere along the way, the road had changed in texture to a yielding surface of baked and compressed red earth. It was cooler, softer, and more welcoming than the bitumen they had left behind. They had not spoken for a long time. His mind wandered. He thought about what she had said about him being about to wet his pants. It brought back memories of his Dalforce days. The rap of her knuckles on his chest jarred him and made him stop.

She pointed to the ground ahead of them. A few feet away, a long, spotted snake uncoiled itself and slithered across the road from their right. It was gone in a few seconds.

She raised her hands and lowered her face into them. Her shoulders slumped. Her neck was coated with grime and sweat. He wished he knew what to say to her. Just when he thought she would break down again, she sighed and straightened up.

"You don't believe in omens, do you?" he said.

"The day they took me away, a snake crossed my path," she mumbled.

She bit her lip and started walking. She shook her head as if she was cursing herself for talking too much.

"Is it the next village?" he said.

She looked at him, head tilted. "Yes," she said. "What do you want to do? You cannot come inside with me. I mean, into my house. I—I want to meet them on my own. It has been a long time, and ..."

Her voice had a lilt that he had not noticed before. "No, I will stay outside," he said.

She let out an exasperated breath.

"I mean," he said, "I will just walk with you to the village and stay outside the village. Not outside your house."

She nodded. He thought she would relapse into silence. She said, "It was such a long way. Time went by so fast, like a stone down a slope. And now it has become so slow. And this pain in my heels— it seems my body is not mine anymore."

"My back hurts, and my heels," he said. "We came a long way."

The rubber plantations had ended, and the pat cut through thick, high grass now. Up in the distance, there was a Ficus tree and a small fish pond.

"Is that where your village starts?" he said.

"Yes," she said. "That is our village pond." Her steps sped up and slowed down. Then she ran, her slippers flapping and kicking up tiny clouds of dust. She reminded him of the boys who had run down to the pool. He could not see her face, but he imagined it lit by a childlike grin and wide, shining eyes. He pushed his gaze away from her buttocks that were thrusting, asserting their roundness against her unshapely black trousers. Just a moment ago, she had been bedraggled and listless. Now she had flown a hundred feet away from him.

He considered running, but even the thought exhausted him. All his joints were sore, but the tendons behind his knees and his heels hurt with a pulsating pain. He trudged on towards her.

She had lowered herself onto her knees first and then got into a squatting position below the large tree. His eyes wandered over her curves again as they accentuated themselves. Her rear was shaped quite like the bottom of a Ficus leaf. When he reached her, he squatted beside her. His calves hurt, but the rest of his body murmured a sigh of relief.

She looked tired. Whatever surge had propelled her here had subsided. She rested her elbows on her inner thighs, brought her knuckles together, and rested her chin on her hands. Her eyes were downcast.

"It looks like rain," she said.

He had not realized that the sky had turned dark. The sun was not scorching his neck any more. There did not seem to be any rain yet where they sat, but a few raindrops lopped onto the surface of the pond, whose still water seemed to push them back before accepting them.

She was looking at him. Her eyes were moist again. Should he reach out and stroke her back?

"Don't worry," she said. "I won't cry."

He chuckled.

She took a deep breath. "You know, the smell of this earth and the tree, and—do you hear the hum of the insects?"

"It's always there," he said. "You hear it when you notice it."

"Yes," she smiled. "I thought it would all come together in a particular way. I thought I could not possibly forget how they all are. And here I am, and it feels different."

"Different how?" he asked.

"I do not know. Dry. All these days, I was … Do you want to know where I was?" There was a catch in her voice.

"No, it's—I know," he said.

"What do you know?"

"I know it will rain soon, so you better move. I'll wait for you here for some time?"

"Why now?"

"What do you mean, why now?"

"I mean, it helped you to have me by your side there, but you don't need me now, right?"

"You keep asking me things I have already told you. I don't have that many places to go to."

"Hmm," she said.

"Why did you come with me?" he said.

"What do you mean, come with you?" She was a bit too loud for his comfort.

"Relax. I mean today—of course, you came with me. On our way here."

"I have nothing. Only what I am wearing, and this, a woman gave me. It seemed better to be with someone. And as you may have noticed, there was no one else coming our way."

He laughed. It was good to be able to.

"You have kind eyes," she said. "All men are bastards, I think you as well. But you have kind eyes."

"Thank you, thank you," he said.

"You know it is true. I am sorry if it is rude."

"Men being bastards? Oh, I know that. That's not what I meant. No one told me about my kind eyes until now."

"It's true," she said. "I don't lie. I do not know how to."

"All women are liars," he said.

Her eyes flashed, and her lips curled combatively. But she let out a hiss and returned to contemplating the pond. He followed her gaze. In the distance, on the far side of the pond, was a single lotus flower, its colour a pink that was fiery as if it had sucked up all the vanishing light.

"That is not true," he said. "I just made it up."

"Do you not have a woman?"

"She's dead," he said.

"I am sorry."

As he stretched his limbs, she was already rising. "I am very sorry," she said again. "I should go now. That is my home." She pointed to the row of huts with attap roofs.

"The second one?"

"No, the third."

"Will you come to let me know all is well? You might as well. I will wait for you."

She looked pensive. "Yes, I will come."

She turned and walked towards the cluster of houses. A deafening thunderclap filled his ears. He looked at the sky. It was still holding up. A gust of wind ruffled the water. The coolness of the air was soothing.

She went slowly up the mud path that ran through the village. A plume of smoke had been curling up from the house in front, but the wind had snuffed it out. Now the village looked ghostly. The woman had shrunk into the distance, but he could still make out her movements, and she smoothed her clothes and removed her hair from her face before climbing the steps that led her home.

The cool wind was still blowing hard. It shook loose heart-shaped leaves from the tree, and they descended onto the ground and the pond in desultory, crooked paths. Water hyacinths had cornered a patch of the pond on the right. The wind bent them and toppled the drops of water they had captured into the pond.

He stood up and stretched. If the skies opened up, the thick tree would only protect him for a while. He considered running to the village and taking shelter below one of the raised floors, like an animal. But it was far, and he might end up embarrassing her.

It was unlikely that the households had pigs, it seemed. Most of the animals, even the village dogs, had disappeared.

The storm blew over as suddenly as it had started. The sun was back again, lower in the sky but no less intense. He pulled his damp shirt apart from his skin in a few places. He turned to look at the village. It was as sleepy as ever. A movement on his left caught his eye.

It was an old woman with sparse grey hair tied in a bun. She walked erect, balancing a basket of tapioca on her head without visible effort. A couple of steps behind her was a young boy carrying a smaller basket, propping it up with a hand. They chattered as they walked but fell silent when they saw Ah Ding. When he smiled at them, the woman's face softened into a weathered smile, and the boy gave him a gap-toothed grin.

He figured they were returning from the market. Business was obviously not very good. He followed them as they sped towards the village, the woman setting a sprightly pace and the boy shuffling to narrow her lead. As Ah Ding stretched lazily to contemplate the pond, there was a slight blur of movement in the path that ran through the village.

It was the woman, his companion on the walk. It struck him only now that he did not know her name. And she did not know his. She descended the steps slowly and then stood with her back to her home. A cry sounded from inside. It must have been very loud to have travelled all the way. He could not make out if it was a child or a woman who had cried out.

The woman stood for a long time before turning to her right, towards the pond. The elderly lady and the boy put their baskets on the ground and gesticulated and jabbered at her. She ignored them and kept walking. The other two fell silent and became still.

She was still far away when she rubbed her sleeves against her cheeks, one by one. Ah Ding looked away. The tiredness had almost left him for a while, but now it descended on him with a vengeance. He felt like lying on his back on the soft, grassy earth.

He wondered why he had not done it earlier. Every joint of his body felt unburdened. The sky had cleared, and its blue fabric peeped through the mesh of branches, drooping roots and Ficus leaves. He wished he could give in to the drowsiness that blanketed him, descend into a sleep that would spare him from talking to her.

The scent of grass and earth, straddled by the thick roots of the tree, brought back memories of the war days. He sat up.

She was walking towards the pond. The old woman and the boy had picked up their baskets, but they stood still, looking at her receding back. A small child came running out into the open space in front of the huts. Ah Ding could not make out if it was a boy or girl. A bent figure in grey swooped down upon it and carried it back indoors.

She walked with her head lowered. Ah Ding turned to contemplate the pond, to reduce the burden of eyes boring into her, for what it mattered.

A blue bird with a long beak dived straight into the pond and fluttered away with something in its mouth, leaving a trail of dripping water and rippling circles in the pond. If it had not happened right before his eyes, if it were not for the whorls on the pond and the delicate splash the bird made as it plunged into the water, he would have thought that he was hallucinating. He imagined the bird chewing the fish and spitting out its bones.

She was close now. He turned to face her. She stood on the path that led back towards the city, her shoulders artificially erect and her gaze vacant. She surveyed the path ahead. A shrill cry pierced the song of the cicadas. It was the child, out again in the clearing in front of the house that had been hers. The child screamed words that lost their meaning in the intervening distance.

She kept her back to the village. Her face fell and she walked slowly to where he stood. Up close, he saw that her eyes were even more puffed than before. She had combed and tied her hair neatly in a bun, though, and she had probably wiped her face and neck.

She sank onto the ground, first in a squatting position and then lowering her buttocks to the ground. Her back was hunched as she wrapped her legs in her arms and rested her chin on her interlocked fingers.

He wanted to tell her that it broke his heart to see her there, that for those few moments, he felt no desire for her, he only wished he could hug her and give her warmth.

"I do not even know your name," he said. "Mine is Ah Ding." As soon as he blurted the words out, he knew it was a stupid thing to say.

She did not seem to have heard him. One moment she was looking into the distance, and the next, without warning, tears ran down her cheeks. She did not bother to wipe them. They flowed into thin, curved streams and dripped onto her hand. She sat motionless and let them flow. When she had exhausted her tears, she wiped her face with her hands and then rested her chin in her hands again.

He had saved his handkerchief, as usual. He had kept his habit of carrying a handkerchief since before the war years. Only, in the intervening period, it had become more symbolic than functional, as he never used it. He reached for it, but it was not easy to fish out. He struggled to his feet, got it, and offered it to her. His lower back screamed out in pain at the sudden movement.

She smiled through her tears and wiped them away with the back of her thick sleeve instead. There was a catch in her breath, but she seemed at peace when she looked into his eyes and announced, "I am done with crying now." She waved away the offered handkerchief.

"I am glad to hear that," he said.

"You must be hungry," she said. "I am sorry I did not get anything for you. I ate very well. Rice and fish, after a long time." She saw him looking at her, thinking about how to reply to that obvious lie, and she grinned. Her teeth were uneven but very white.

He said, "After a meal like that, you must feel like a kopi, no? I am sorry there isn't one here."

She laughed, and he felt happy for her. The sleepiness returned to him. It was more intense this time.

"I need to lie down for some time," he said.

"Here?"

"Where else?"

He lay down again on the soft earth, not caring for his clothes. Her presence next to him was soothing.

*

The sun on his face woke him up. It was a much mellower sun, but it had been baking him for some time.

He had kicked off his sandals, rolled over on his left, and used his arm as a cushion. He must have slept a long time. The woman was standing by the pond. She bent to pick up a flat stone and threw it so that it hit the water at a tangent. It skidded smartly twice before plonking into the depths of the pond. A patter sounded from somewhere. It was the boy who had walked by with the vegetable basket earlier. He was clapping.

The boy picked up a stone and mimicked her. His throw did not seem different, but his stone sank without a trace, and he raised his hands to his head in mock anguish. Then he saw Ah Ding and blushed. He gave them both a wave and ran off towards the huts.

She started walking towards him. Her feet were bare. They were incredibly pale, he thought.

He looked at his own callused feet, with their veins sticking out and overgrown nails. These feet had carried him quite far today. It was the furthest he had walked since the day, in 1942, when they had all been told to report for screening after the British surrender.

Her feet were thin and delicate, like the rest of her. As she drew nearer, he saw that a scar ran through her right foot, almost all the way from her big toe to the arch of her foot.

She saw him looking at it, and the glimmer of a smile on her face vanished. She turned away abruptly to face the pond, her arms stiff by her side.

He got to his feet. The rest had done him wonders. She turned her head a bit towards him but did not face him. He walked to her side. The sun was still high over the treetops, but they had only an hour or so before sunset.

"I was very tired," he said.

She smiled. She must have washed her face. The streaks of tears had disappeared. How could she not be exhausted?

"I was about to wake you up," she said. "I need to go."

"Where will you go?"

Her eyes turned cold. "I will go on my own. Back to Bukit Panjang Circus, and from there, bus number 2 to the city."

"And you know someone in the city?"

"Yes." She gulped.

She was lying. She had been right. She could not tell a lie. What would happen to her in the city of dogs?

"They gave me—I have money," she said.

"What type? How much?" he asked. She looked blank. He sighed and said, "If it is banana money, Japanese, it may work today and a few more days. But it is Japanese. It will not work later. It will be useless. Pieces of paper."

Her face fell.

He had been thinking this through for a while, in his half-sleep, but it came together now. "You need a roof over your head and food to eat. And even to earn a bit. I know the place. They cannot say no to me. The old lady who runs it, I mean."

She frowned at him. She was trying to make out what he was leading to. "I have a little money. I can give it to you. It's not much." There was no point in telling her it was the only note he had.

Her eyes burned bright, and she drew up her shoulders. "I won't do it," she said.

"What?" he said. "Oh. No, that's not what I meant." He looked at his toes. They were curled upwards. "I—I sometimes went to the house in Jalan Jurong Kechil. My Japanese boss sent me there, and I got a free ticket. I came to you. I, I just sat there."

She lowered her eyes. She sat down slowly in the same position she had taken earlier, squatting, with her chin resting on her hands.

He wondered if she would cry again. When she spoke, her voice was hoarse but controlled. "When did you recognize me?"

"It does not matter," he said. "I don't remember exactly when. Not when we met in the morning. And I don't go around asking women if I have met them before, by the way."

She looked at him and half-smiled. "What do you want from me if it is not to sleep with me?"

"Today, nothing more," he said. "It's not much of a life I have, some would say, but I quite like it. For now, it is enough that I had you with me today. It probably saved my life. Here, take this." He pulled his thin, worn wallet out from his back pocket and picked out the neatly folded ten-dollar note. She looked doubtfully at him. The light had turned pale. The jaded purple of the note took on a reddish tinge. "Take it before I take it back," he said.

"I don't know how," she said.

"Take it in your hands," he said. "How else?"

She took it with both hands. "I will work," she said. "I will not sell myself. I will return this to you and still remain in your debt."

"Yes, I know," he said. "I know you, I mean. There is a beehoon place near the big Kwan Im Temple. The woman who runs it owes me her life. She can do with a hand. If you work for her, it may be a hard life, but you will be fine."

She was still sitting, holding the note in her hands. She got up and put it in the pocket of her trousers, gingerly.

"Do you want my Japanese money?" she asked.

"No, I have a bit. I'll let you know if I need it on the way. Maybe to buy tickets."

"Tickets?"

"In the bus. We should go now, before it gets too dark. If we can get a trishaw to Bukit Panjang Circus, we'll take it at the market. It's all right to take one now, in the dark. I didn't want to risk taking it in the daytime. Then like you said, we need to get bus number 2. I'm sure there will be at least one bus if we leave now."

"This shop, the beehoon place, will you take me there?"

"Yes."

She mumbled.

"What?" he said.

"I don't know how to …" She pressed her lips together.

"Then don't."

Her face softened. She said, "Do you know, when you were sleeping, you were talking to yourself, nodding your head. Moving your hand. Like this." She held her arm vertical, opened her palm and rotated it. "Like you were thinking about something." She smiled.

"Was I?"

She nodded. "Thank you. I will not forget you. I will not forget this moment."

"Let's go."

They started off. She looked to her right, towards her village, for just a second, as if she did not want him to catch her looking that way.

*

The trishaw driver had stood on his pedals to get them up the slope to the hump at the market. His taut shins had bulged with the effort, and he wheezed with every stroke. His stench had filled Ah Ding's nostrils for a while before he grew used to it. The cool air was a balm to his body. She must be even more tired than him. He hoped she had not started her day as early as him. Her closeness, the rub of her shoulder and thigh as they were jostled along, prickled him. She had been subdued on the way back. At the Malay kampung, she had stopped for a minute by a palm tree, placing her hand on its trunk. Did it remind her of the one in front of her home? It had a similar curved trunk, but so did many others.

She had perked up like a child when he hailed a trishaw. He had not bothered to ask about the price. There were more people on the other side of the road, though both sides were crowded. "Listen," he said to her. "Shift to the other side." He pointed to the right side of the trishaw, and he walked over to the left. She moved over. She sat with her hands clasped tight. Her eyes were bright. It made him want to squeeze her to him. He had to haul himself up with both aching hands. The seat cushion was hard, filled with coir and patchily covered with a rough, discoloured cloth. But he felt like a king, with her beside him.

The trishaw tipped over the hump, and the driver sat back, making the most of the downward slope. They picked up speed, and he honked his dull, red-coloured horn. He had to swerve to avoid a crawling bullock cart. It threw the woman against Ah Ding. She leaned away immediately. The moist evening air fanned him. The scents of a flower shop stayed for a moment. She took a deep breath at the same time as he did. They smiled at each other. The twilight, accentuated by the gas lanterns in some of the shops and houses, played on her face. He considered asking her name but let the thought drift away. There was plenty of time.

They were at Bukit Panjang Circus, and the driver turned the trishaw at a breakneck speed, humming a Malay tune. His biceps strained as he clamped on the brakes, but the brakes were obviously worn out, and he overshot the Green Bus Company stop by a few feet. There were two others waiting for the bus, an elderly woman and a fat man, probably her son.

Ah Ding asked the driver how much. The man sized up his passengers before asking for five dollars. Her eyebrows rose, and she was ready to argue, but Ah Ding quickly took out a ten-dollar banana note and flicked it over. The driver was still panting. Ah Ding got off. He winced as his feet and shins stung with the impact. He motioned for her to get off on the left side.

"Won't you take back the change?" she asked.

"No," he said.

The driver's teeth shone. "Thank you!" he shouted and set off. He sang a few lines of Kimigayo before laughing and switching to a Malay song.

"You have so much money? Some much that you can throw it around?" she asked.

"Oh, that's no problem. I liked the ride."

She snuggled up to him before the shock set in, and she stepped back, embarrassed. "It was wonderful," she said. The street light was dim, but he thought he saw her blush. "I felt I was flying!"

"Have you never been on one of those before?"

"Never."

"I enjoyed being on the downslope. By the way, that was banana money I gave him—make sure you don't forget. It will become useless pretty soon."

"What I have also? All of it?"

"Yes, why else do you think I told you?"

Her face morphed into a frown.

"I wonder if they know. I hope they do."

"Your people?"

"My—yes."

The honk of the bus carried from beyond visible range before its whining engine was audible. Then its lights blinded them. The old woman and her companion were first to the door, blocking the way of a couple of men who wanted to get off.

"Aiyah! Let them get down first!" the conductor shouted. The exiting passengers shoved their way through.

Ah Ding offered her his hand once he was on the first step. It was a high step, and his calve hurt. She was not looking. She had already clamped the grip on the door to pull herself up. The bus was more than half full. Ah Ding scanned the seats and moved quickly to take the ones next to the driver. That was his favourite spot. He let her take the window seat.

The bus pulled away, and the conductor swooped down on them. She reached for her money, but Ah Ding made a stopping sign with his hand. He paid for two tickets to the depot with the banana money and took the change back.

It was hard to talk with the bedlam of the engine next to them. They were right beside the grey hood that covered the massive engine. It reeked of burning charcoal. It took Ah Ding a while to figure out what was special about the front of the bus. It was spotless, which was quite remarkable for a Green Bus. The hood, the windscreen and the rear-view mirror were polished and gleaming, much in contrast to the seats and the windows. The bus driver was a bespectacled man who mumbled to himself and kept looking at his side mirror. He drove with a practised swagger, mostly keeping his right hand on the wheel. His left hand either goaded the gear stick or dangled around. The lights on Upper Bukit Timah Road blurred into streaks as the bus gobbled up the distance.

She smiled at him. "Imagine if we had got one in the morning. So fast!" Her teeth showed.

He smiled back. "Is this your first time as well? In a bus?"

Her smile vanished. "No! I've been many times. What do you think? Kampung girls don't go in buses? And those buses were even faster. They had different engines then!"

He shrugged. "Yes, they had diesel engines. These days, it's charcoal. Most of the buses have stopped, anyway."

She pursed her lips, satisfied that she had defended her honour. She turned to look outside. The wind had shaken a few strands of her hair loose. She brushed it from her forehead with her fingers. She caught him staring at her, and he looked away.

In the rear mirror, he saw the two communists in the middle row, on the right side. The leader sat with his arms folded, looking straight ahead. The other man leaned towards him, almost speaking into his ears. Ah Ding clenched his fingers to prevent his hands from trembling.

They had already crossed the fire station and the shrine.

"Is something wrong again?" she asked. Her cheekbones glowed in the pale light of the bus. Behind her, the streaks of light thickened into blobs as the bus slowed down in front of Beauty World. The bright, throbbing lights on their left bathed the bus in shades of red and blue. Bars of the song that he would later recognize at Gong Xi Gong Xi filtered in through the windows.

This was where they had started, and it made sense to part around here.

A swarm of people had climbed on board. A young couple stood next to them, their faces flushed. They looked at each other in the way that unjaded love inspires people to. For so many people, today was the start of a new life, an unfettered one. He was not so sure that things would get better for them all, though, without first getting worse.

For him, there was no doubt—he would be lucky to live through this time.

He felt the squeeze of her fingers on his wrist. "What is wrong?"

The driver engaged the giant gear lever and performed a series of steps with his hands and feet. Smoke rose from the engine in front. With a weak roar, the bus trundled forward and settled into an accelerating motion.

"They are here. In the bus," he said.

"The men you are running from?" she asked.

"Yes."

She closed her eyes and looked at her palms, which lay lifeless on her lap. She spoke into his ear. "What do you want to do? Have they seen you?"

"No, they haven't, and with this crowd, I should be safe for some time. But I will not stay with you till the end, till the bus depot. I will get off before Newton Circus. Maybe around Botanic Garden. I can't be here once the crowd has thinned."

She pressed her lips together and closed her eyes. "Where will I go? Should I come with you?"

He felt ashamed that he had not spared a thought for her.

"Shouldn't you keep the money you gave me? The British money?"

He looked into her eyes. It was true, he thought. She had a good soul, this woman. She was not capable of deceit. It could get her very far in life if she was with the right people. Or it could be her undoing. God knew.

"No, keep it. I gave it to you. I think I got away again because I was with you." He smiled. "If they get me now and you are with me, I don't know—it may not be good for you."

She gulped.

"Don't worry," he said. "Nothing has changed for you. You get off at the last stop before the depot. It will still be lively in that part. All you have to do is ask for Waterloo Street and the beehoon place next to the Kwan Im Temple. It's roughly like this: you will get off at the last stop. When you get off, walk opposite to the direction in which the bus was moving. You will come to a road, Middle Street. Got that?"

"Yes." She hung on to every word.

"Cross it, then on your right, you will see Waterloo Street. Waterloo. Kwan Im Temple. Beehoon shop. The lady's name is Lai. The shop is Fatt Kee Shou Shi. To Lai, you have to say, 'A frog jumps into the pond.' Say these words."

She repeated them.

"Say them again."

She pursed her lips in disapproval, but he bored into her eyes. She said all the words. She was close enough that her lips seemed to tickle the side of his left ear.

"Why that line about the frog?" she asked.

"God knows. Someone else chose it, not me. What will you do if these two question you?"

She stiffened, and her eyes dilated. She squeezed his wrist again.

"Don't worry, it won't happen, I think. I will ask this woman to sit next to you. They will not have seen me with you, even if they catch me. But what if they do question you? What will you say?" he gently pulled her hand away from his wrist. She blushed. Was it the first time her dimples had appeared? Or could he have been stupid enough to not have noticed them earlier? He wanted to lean forward and kiss her on her forehead. He imagined her skin on his lips.

She was looking at him like a child waiting to be told a story. He said, "Do what you are good at. Tell them the truth. Look them in the eyes. Tell them where you were, that you were forced. That house is called a comfort house, outside, by the way. Tell them I told you that. Say that I asked you to be with me. That you felt safer also. That your family turned you away. Understand? Only say one lie. Say that your cousin runs a beehoon shop, and that is the only place you can go."

She nodded. "Don't ask me to repeat that," she said.

He chuckled. She sank her head into her palms.

He leaned closer. "I hope you are not going to cry again."

"No. I will never cry again." She was wrong, of course. There is no woman who does not cry. Fake tears or real ones. Born woman, have to cry.

The din of the bus engine and the rattling of the windows had given them the best possible cover to talk without being heard. Now they were on a crowded stretch of Bukit Timah Road. The driver slowed the bus down and made liberal use of his horn.

She interlocked her fingers and bowed to him. Her lips moved, but no sound came out.

"What?" he asked.

"I do not know why you are doing this," she said.

"Nor do I."

"I do not know how to thank you."

He stayed quiet.

"I will pray for you," she said. Her eyes were moist, but her voice was steady. "I will ask Kwan Im to bless you."

"She knows all about me. What are the chances? Why don't you bless me instead?"

"Did you say that to make me cry?"

He laughed. The bus was less crowded already. It was time to go. The screeching of the brakes had started. "I'm off," he told her. Their hands met and squeezed each other. He pulled away. As he got up, he nodded politely to the young couple and gestured for the girl to sit in his place. She bowed and sat down in a jiffy, taking her eyes off her lover only for a second.

He kept his face towards the door and scanned the rest of the bus. The communists seemed to be sleeping. There was something niggling him—something he was forgetting.

The bus had stopped. He pushed his way ahead of an old man waiting to climb down from the other side of the aisle. He opened the door latch and lowered himself down gingerly, remembering the experience of stepping down from the trishaw. The crowd behind him propelled him forward onto the high sidewalk. He kept his back to the bus and bent down as if to adjust his sandals. He felt her eyes on him but kept his eyes on his dust-covered toes.

When he stood up, his head swam. He gripped the street pole to steady himself. It was warm. The night air was scented with frangipani.

He nodded to himself as he remembered what it was that had been on his mind. He had not asked her name.

5

Hate at First Sight

2005, Ah Ding

I T IS HATE AT FIRST SIGHT. She is too much like a Channel U star, one of those girls who advertise for Japanese skin creams in the displays at bus stops and everywhere. Much later, there will be a time when I ask her how come our girls became taller, fairer and grew bigger breasts. Did it have something to do with the economy? She will laugh it off.

Anyway, she sits there the day we first met, her hands clasped in her lap, smiling at me and probably wondering how she landed up in my place. Her toes are curled with tension. My home is … well, it has been home for many years now. It is a short bus ride away from where I work. Oh yes, it is work. It is not easy money. Think about going up to people who are stuffing themselves and asking them if they will buy tissues from you. Even the Ang Mohs will crinkle their noses as if you stink. And these days, there are too many bloody Mainland Chinese and India Indians, anyway.

But that's not the point. I was saying, my house is how it is. Since that guy, Sanwan, left and I have it to myself, it is less smelly. Before you ask, left as in he went missing. Went out and did not come back. Where is he now, how did he disappear from this small island? How the fuck do I know?

So anyway, she only has me to deal with, and I take a shower every day. Even when I lived outside, I went to the public toilets and took a shower at five in the morning. It's something that Mr Cheng drilled into us, bless that interfering asshole's soul. When she came in, she stood there, a bit lost, in her dazzling white T-shirt and her knee-length shorts. She is pretty. The thing is, at eighty-two, I can look at a girl without undressing her in my mind, imagining the shades of her pointed nipples and the size of her aureoles. If I had reached this stage earlier, life would have been smoother. A lot less of my semen would have to be filtered out of the NEWater that people like you, people who read books, pay for.

"So how, Uncle?" she says. "It's my first day doing this."

"First day?"

"Hmm. Volunteering," she says. "Are you sure it's okay if I sit?" I tell her to sit on the one chair I have. I have my butt on the floor and my back against the wall.

"I told you it's all right. I only have that one chair," I say.

"Maybe we should get you another chair?"

"What will I do with it? I only got one butt."

She laughs, covering her mouth with the back of her hand. "Well, for the times I come. It will mostly be Monday evenings. The market is closed, right?"

"Yes. Tell me, what do you really want out of this? Do they pay you?"

"I—What's that gash? On your head?"

"Oh, I just hurt myself." I touch the right side of my bald head. The wound has not completely gone.

"But how did you get it? Did someone …?"

"Don't be silly," I say.

"Then how?" she asks.

In the dream, I had stood looking out on Stamford Road through a bamboo blind on an arched window of the East District Branch. A solitary, squat Japanese truck trundled along the deserted road noiselessly. I focused my hearing on the irregular creaking of the fan. Oishi gripped my chin and turned my face towards the woman. Her finger was broken, bent backwards. The soldier tossed the pliers aside on the table and stepped back. A single tear streaked her chin. She nodded her head again and again without stopping until I was jolted from my sleep. "Sleeping, that's how. I don't know what I did in my sleep, just banged my head somehow. Maybe I had a dream. God knows what I was up to in my sleep."

She looks around the room. Her voice is small, her forehead furrowed. "You sleep on the floor?"

"Where else? You sleep on the roof or what?"

She laughs again, this time without covering her mouth. One of her teeth has a metallic look. Her eyes dance. She rocks back and forth. "We'll get you a tilam, a mattress. I'll ask if it's possible."

"Don't bother."

"No bother, I think they have old ones. It's nothing. Did you have something to put on the wound? Betadine?"

I chuckle. "Betadine? No, I just pressed a cloth on it. It was okay. Anyway, it was nothing much."

She pulls out her phone, a fancy wide one with many buttons, and punches its keys with her two thumbs. "I'm making a note," she said. "About the mattress."

"You need your phone to make a note?"

"Haha, it's an N70. What's the point of having it if I don't show it? Ah … there's a reply. I think they have a mattress. It will be a used one, of course."

"You didn't tell me why you are here with this company. What is it?" I say.

"KFA. Keeping Faith Alive."

"Funny name."

She puts her knuckles on the sides of her hips and purses her lips in mock anger. "So, this is how you thank us?"

"Well, that's how it is. You end up cranky when you become an old man, see?"

"I won't have that problem, thankfully."

"No. But I sometimes say, better old than dead."

"No, don't say that."

"So one more time, why do you do this?"

"You really are a suspicious old uncle."

"Like I said, better old than dead."

Her face changes as if she has taken off a mask. "I do it because I gain from it," she says.

"Gain how? They pay you?"

"No, it's not volunteering if they pay me. I do it because it makes me look good."

"You look good, anyway. Did you study well?"

"Okay, not bad. I went to Poly. Then got a degree."

"So what do you gain if they don't pay you?"

She lets out an exaggerated sigh. "I told you already, what? It makes me look good."

"How does that help?"

"Well, when I apply for my next job, it might help."

"I still don't understand."

"Now I know why they told me you are an old fart," she says and gives me a pleasant, toothy smile.

I am shaking with laughter. I have fallen for her, although I know she has told me most of the truth, but not all of it. Of course, I never tell her, but for the next five weeks, I will count the minutes as I wait for her to knock on the door every Monday at six in the evening. The worse my sleeplessness gets, the more relaxing I will find her company.

"There's nothing not to understand. Whenever I apply next for a job, I'll write that I did some good work by volunteering. It's wayang. The people who read my application know I did it to score some more points, and I know they know. I get some credit points, that's all. Everyone is happy, including you, Uncle."

I like how honest she is. "Isn't it better for them to send girls to flats that have women?" I say.

"I guess it is. I didn't ask, and they didn't tell me. I have three flats to visit. Next, there may be two of us. I don't know."

I nod and lower my head. When she leaves, I struggle to my feet and walk to the door. I wait at the door till she waves me inside from in front of the lift. The lights are on in the corridor, and I can only see her silhouette. I am quite sure she is giving me her toothy smile.

*

It is a Seahorse mattress with a couple of faded stains. The two guys who come with it call me first. They don't look around my flat and don't say a word. They just put it leaning against the wall. One of them waves, and they are out. As soon as they have gone, I lower the side of the mattress to the floor. It is heavy. It will take some strength to lower it and put it back up against the wall. I lie on it and stretch my hands and legs. It is surprisingly stiff. It strikes me that I could fall off it. But maybe not. People don't fall out of their beds, or I would have heard of it. What if Sanwan comes back? He won't be getting his arse on this, for sure. It is all mine.

I feel a pang of shame. What the hell? If I'm not around, of course, he can sleep on it if he takes a shower first. There are plenty of places where people take their turns to sleep.

As I lie there, I fight off sleep. It is way too early. I think I could go down to the void deck. I wake up at four in the morning, every morning. My mind and body got used to it back in the days when I was living outside. Now it suits me quite fine. I'm at the market early. I take the first bus at 5:45.

I usually lie down at nine, and sleep comes when it comes. Before I met that woman with no name, I could count on it coming. Now it is different. Much earlier, I used to kill the insects, the ones that disturbed my sleep. I kept a slipper handy. Later, I kind of reconciled myself to being with them. Maybe I just got lazy.

I stretch on the mattress. I push my limbs towards its four corners and still don't touch the ends. I roll on my right and my left.

I have not slept two nights in a row. That evening, sleep overpowers me.

Sometimes, when it rains hard, they say it's raining like the end of the world, although it happens very often here. I got caught in that kind of rain last week. I was walking along the street, a few hundred feet away from cover. The air turned cold, and the skies opened up in a matter of minutes. I knew there was nothing to do but give in, let the rain soak and cleanse me. I turned my face up, and the big drops massaged my eyelids. A streak of lightning turned the sky pale, and the giant-sized blue numbers on the side of the block, 106, glowed.

The sleep that descends on me that first time on the mattress is as overpowering as that rain. I stretch in my sleep and marvel in my sleep at the many ways in which my old body can arrange itself. When I wake up, I have memories of the many dreams I had. I dreamt of a scented, moonlit forest and a pretty girl. By the time I get up and get my 3-in-1 coffee, the dreams will have faded away.

I always dream in bright colours these days. As my eyes grow dimmer, my dreams turn brighter, and they exhaust me. Last night, though, my dreams were silvery. When I woke up, my vision cleared in an instant. I never felt so refreshed.

A mattress is a wonderful thing, I think as I sip the scalding coffee.

*

"Is that what you will eat all week?" she asks. "You could change the flavour at least, no?"

"What does it matter?" I say. I would not have allowed anyone else to poke around in the fridge and cupboard.

She came a bit early that evening. I have taken to skipping my evening round of the void deck and the coffee shop in Block 107 on Mondays. I get back, put the wheelchair in a corner next to the laundry bucket, and wait for her. I sit on the mattress, sometimes playing the snake game on my phone. I have to hold the phone far away. I leave the gate and the door open.

She sits down, and we talk for a while. She wants to get something off her chest. When she blurts it out, I do not have the heart to say no. "Uncle, your place needs cleaning," she says. She presses her lips in a kind of grimace as if it hurts to say such a rude thing.

She gets up and opens her shoulder bag. Out come a couple of cloth pieces and a sponge. "Today, I'll just do this area." She points to the side that had the slab and the cooking area. She walks over to the slab, runs her pointing finger on it, and smiles as she shows me the dust on the tip of the finger.

"Thank you for not using the middle finger," I say.

She rocks as she laughs. "Come help me," she says after she has recovered. "Don't just sit there. Do you want me to help you up?"

I wave her aside. It takes me time to get up. My hands used to be stronger, what with all the navigating they did on the wheelchair. Since I met that woman, the one from sixty years ago, I sometimes feel they have lost some of their power. But things aren't that bad yet. We are done quite soon. We have to wring the wipers quite a few times under the taps.

"That will do for today," she says. She takes the wipers and lays them over the sink to dry.

She looks inside my fridge. It is one of those days when it is on the empty side. Sometimes, I have a packet of food from the market. I decide I will get a drink for her next time. In the cupboard, there are only packets of Maggi.

"Won't you get bored with Maggi Chicken flavour?" she says in a half-scolding tone. "At least you could have got different flavours."

"Oh no, I won't get bored. If I do, I get Nissin."

She rolls her eyes. "But the market has great food," she says. She bites her lip as she figures that what makes me live on Maggi is probably not a great love of its flavour. "I'll get some fruit next time," she adds.

"You are too nice," I said. "I am lucky to know you."

"I enjoy doing this. And by the way, what I told you the other day about why I do this, I never said that to anyone else."

I wonder why she is telling me that.

"So what do you want me to get next time, cut fruit or juice?"

I shrug. "My stomach can't take all that stuff. It's a waste of money, I think. When I can, I get stuff like carrot cake or char kway teow.

"Uncle, you got to eat well. How will you grow if you don't eat properly? I'll get you fruit."

I have to laugh. "You are a good girl," I said. "Are you also good to your parents?"

Her eyes flash for a second. She clears her throat, and that is signal enough for me to keep away from that subject.

"Has anyone told you that you have kind eyes?"

"How can eyes be kind?" I say. I do have a feeling that someone used that exact phrase sometime, somewhere. It is hard to sort the tangled threads of my experiences.

*

The next time, she brings me a packet of cut fruit in a plastic box. She puts it in the fridge as soon as she comes in and refuses to open it. She makes me promise to finish it in two days. It was cheap, she says, at Fairprice.

"Where did you grow up?" She asks me all of a sudden.

I clear my throat like she did when I asked about her parents. "It was a different life. Singapore was nothing like this. I was in a small village."

"Were you there in the Second World War times? Was it hard? I read some incredible stories."

I sigh. "I was there, I was there. But now it feels like a different birth. In between, many things happened. There was a commotion around 1965. Riots. That guy, what's-his-name, Sukarno, had some crazy ideas. And for a while, I was in prison—did you know that?"

She nods her head to say yes. She never asks me about the past again. She is smart. If she did ask, I do not know what I would do. My bad dreams have returned. The mattress cushions me from the floor, not from the bruises those dreams give me.

*

The numbers of the block, 106, are as big as two storeys. In the evening light, their blue stands out against the pale cream colour of the tower. I am tempted to just fold up the wheelchair and walk up the steps. It would be shorter, and most people who matter already know that the wheelchair is a necessary wayang in my line of work.

Zhu Hua—that is her name—asked me about it with a twinkle in her eye. "That wheelchair you have in the corner, Uncle, was that your own idea?"

I shook my head. "There is no such thing as *own idea*," I said. "Anyway, all ideas are borrowed."

She tilted her head and raised an eyebrow as if to acknowledge an exceptionally wise remark, which it was.

"I saw one guy when I started off, at the crossing near Tiong Bahru Plaza. He had a sign saying 'Every Dog Has Its Day'. Now that is sad. What I do, like my boss used to say, is keep my customers in mind."

"He was a smart man, was your boss," she said. "Where was this?"

"A moving company that employed ex-convicts. My back gave way, and the bills were too high."

Her smile froze, and she gulped. "I am sorry," she said.

"It's not your fault," I told her.

She smiled again. "No."

Now I stand there, debating whether to fold up the chair. Strangely, after all these years, I still feel awkward about doing it in public. The bus stop is quite deserted, but I always feel eyes on me from Block 106 or the overbridge on the right.

I give up. I wheel myself along the pavement. It is quite a distance, and a lot of it is uphill, but I am used to it. On the way, I think of the lady from HDB. She is a nice woman. She hated the words she had to pass on. But she got them out, anyway. They will have to evict me if I do not clear the rent. It is very low, the rent, if I keep paying it on time. And there is this problem with the missing guy who is supposed to share the flat. Her face flushed, and her breath became shallow as if she was deeply ashamed of what she was doing.

I told her it would be all right.

There is a reason why there are pawnbrokers here and not in the market where I work.

My arms are aching a bit by the time I get to the lift lobby. Since that woman, the one whose name I do not know, recognized me, I have lost strength each day. When I finally get home, I am out of the wheelchair the moment I close the door behind me. I stretch, and my back immediately feels better. I put the bag of tissues away in a corner of the cupboard, above the sink.

I take out the box of green tea bags and put it conspicuously on the slab. I look at myself in the mirror in the bathroom.

It is not the mirror's fault, I tell myself. My lips languidly curl into a smile. I brush my thin hair into place.

I walk about a bit before lying down on the mattress. Earlier, I would take out my 3310 and play the snake game on it. The thing about lying down at this time is that it is very hard to fight off sleep. It is a miracle that there are no bedbugs, I reflect, at least not yet. From what I have heard, I am one of the lucky ones in the block.

I am in the twilight between wakefulness and sleep when the knock comes. I scramble up and tell her to come in. She knows that both the gate and the door are kept open for her.

"Were you sleeping? At this time?" Her forehead is furrowed in disbelief.

"Have mattress, will sleep," I say. The dreams are getting worse. Last night, it was a man getting the drowning treatment. I woke up crying.

She rolls her eyes for dramatic effect. "Here, I got some custard apple and jackfruit," she says. "But what's this?"

"I got it," I say. I felt a flush rising in my cheeks. It is a strange feeling.

"Oh, that's—that's great!" she says. "I'll put the fruits in the fridge. Is this from the market, from the prawn mee stall with the long lines? Oh, and you've got green tea as well! Nice!" She moves quickly to fill the kettle with water and switch it on. I think of all that is new in the house—the mattress with a new fitted sheet, the mirror, the water filter, fruits once a week. There are things I have firmly refused to take, like pillows and a rice cooker.

She sits on the chair as usual, and I, on the mattress. I make the prawn mee last, every bit of it, but she wolfs it down in a few minutes.

"What?" she says.

"You're supposed to chew on it," I say.

"Eh, it's just too tasty. Thank you, thank you, Uncle."

"You can call me Ah Ding."

"No, Uncle is fine," she says. We sip the tea. It is perfect for washing down the greasy mee. I try to keep my burp soft. I pray that I will not fart. When I am alone, it is a welcome relief, but it would be awkward with her in the room. I am sure she will laugh it off, but I am happier that my stomach holds up. The thick, salty smell of the mee still lingers in the room, and the last of the tea caresses my throat.

"I got something for you," she says. "Guess what?"

"I'm no good at guessing," I say.

"Dan-tan!" she sings. She reaches into her shoulder bag. Her smile vanishes for a while, replaced by a sheepish frown, as she forages inside. She smiles again when she takes out a bright yellow thing in a plastic pack.

"What is it?" I ask as she steps forward and places it into my hands with both of hers.

"Do you really not know?"

I have guessed.

"It's a cover for your old 3310! It will look much better. Don't say you don't like it. Please?"

I do not know what to say.

"Please?" she says again. Her face lengthens a bit, and her smile contracts.

I tell her, in halting words, about the phone. It wasn't much use to me anyway, though I will miss playing the snake game. I actually haven't got a single call on it in the last month, except the couple from HDB. And I have used the money to clear the rent. I tell her that they are nice enough and probably wouldn't evict me out onto the street. But I don't even want to move to another place. "And now I have the mattress to worry about," I tell her with a sheepish smile.

She squats on the floor in front of me. For once, she has nothing to say.

"I'll keep it anyway," I say. "When I buy my next phone, it will probably be a 3310 as well."

"I thought very hard about what to get you." She speaks in a small voice.

I pat her shoulder. I feel no lust. It is very liberating. I only wish it had happened earlier.

"It was an excellent idea," I say. "It won't spoil."

She snaps her fingers. "I'll ask them to get you a phone!" She leans forward eagerly.

"No, don't worry. I'll get one in a few months. If I don't, you can get it on my next birthday, in January."

Life works in strange ways. That moment, when I like her more than ever, is when I remember where I have seen her before. She was coming down the escalator with the woman whose name I did not know, the one whom I met all those years ago. Zhu Hua has coloured her hair since then. Did she do it to make sure I wouldn't recognize her?

"I know where I saw you," I say.

She tilts her head. "Saw me?"

"I saw you with that woman, you know who I mean. I don't know her name. So she sent you here? What did she tell you about me? Is that why you asked about the war years?"

She lowers herself down and squats on the floor. She crosses her legs and puts her chin between her knees. "She just told me she owed you a lot, that you were kind to her. And she is right. I meant it when I told you that you have kind eyes."

I push myself up. My knees have no strength, and I wheeze with effort. I put a hand on the wall to steady myself. Then I walk to the window.

It is dark outside. The blue and yellow of the opposite block of flats, 107, has melted into a colourless pattern of rectangles, interrupted by lights in most of the apartments. By day, the clothes hanging from the poles have every possible colour in the world. At night, they are dyed into shades of grey.

In the small gap between blocks, the trees that reach up to the seventh floor are still. The air is warm after a blistering dry day. Somewhere on the right, a lucky family is frying fish for dinner.

"Are you angry with me?" she says.

I am tired, very tired. I turn around slowly. She is pensive and wide-eyed. "Will she be angry with you? If I tell you not to come here?"

She presses her lips and gulps. "I will be unhappy. Doesn't that matter? I like coming here. Why is it important that she wanted me to? She just found out how to help you. But it does me good as well."

"What is she to you?"

"She's my aunt."

"I see."

"She means it from the bottom of her heart. She has a lot to thank you for. I know her very well. She is a very straightforward person. Like me. She just wants to do what she can for you."

All she has done is bring back memories of hell. "The best thing is to leave me alone. I am done with my life, and it is time for me to face the gods now. Yama and Shangti. Do you know them?"

"I think so. The gods of death and justice."

"Hmm. And I do not want to have anything to do with my past in the few remaining days. Not that past. Is that clear?"

Her lips quiver. I hope she will not cry because it will not change my mind, but will definitely mess it. She does not. "Can I not come back next week? Is that what you are saying?"

"Not next week."

She nods. "If you do not want me, I shouldn't come. Shall I ask them to send someone else to look in?"

"I like you," I say. "Look at me." She looks into my eyes. I say, "I like you a lot. You are a good girl, like your aunt. I am sorry about this.

"I need to forget some things. They don't let me sleep, after all these years, if I don't completely wipe them away from my mind. That's why you cannot come."

She says, "You are a kind man. You have kind eyes and a kind soul. I feel it. She was right. I wish I could do more for you. There are ways. You could go to a counsellor. There are doctors, specialists in these things."

"Those ways are not for me."

"You don't even have a phone now. I can't call you. What if you need help?"

"I'll go to the neighbours." I smile.

"I will come to the market to see that you are okay, sometimes. Is that okay?"

"Okay," I say. I don't say that the market is a public place, anyway. "Don't forget to buy tissues from me. And I'm keeping the mattress."

She shakes her head in resignation. "I'll come every day."

"It's closed on Mondays."

"I know." She smiles.

*

The crack in the paint on the roof has grown. The girl in the next flat is wailing. I lie on my back, forcing myself to avoid turning. I try to imagine the snake game to take my mind away from those years that I wanted to erase. She talked about kind eyes, that girl. But Singapore in those years was no place for kind men.

6

The Moving Finger Writes

1942, Ah Ding

Telok Kurau School Screening Camp, 18 February 1942, three days after the surrender of Singapore to the Japanese Army

THE SUN SHONE bright and hard. Inside the van, it was dark and clammy. Ah Ding wanted to burst out. He felt choked as if he was back in the dream that had woken him up early. In his dream, Fusang's cheongsam—a blue floral one that he had only fantasized about, never seen her in—had enveloped him. He smelled the scent of her sweat and felt himself harden. Then the dress had pressed on all of him. His hands were trapped by his side, and his chest hurt as his lungs strained against the unyielding sheath. He shivered for a long time after he woke up, drenched. When he held his face, his palms became wet.

He thought of Fusang now, Fusang, who had lain stony-eyed while her body was jerked up and down. When it was over, the light had left her eyes. He knew what would help him break free now. Yes. A scream. He wished he could scream from his gut, scream so that the whole conquered city heard him.

Colonel Oishi would turn towards him. Colonel Oishi, who reflected the rising sun from many spots around his immaculate presence. From the band around his peaked cap, from his spotless spectacles, from his three polished belts, the brass buttons on his tunic. From the hilt of his sabre, from his glistening knee-length boots. From the air around him. Colonel Oishi's eyes would bear the mild reproach that Ah Ding had seen when the Colonel burst a prisoner's eardrum. A flicker of disappointment at having to descend to the level of beasts to deal with beasts.

Ah Ding knew he would not scream. His nails bit into his palms. He had thought the hood over his head would comfort him while the rest of the men cowered before the Kempeitai, the Japanese military police. Now he felt naked. What if his shirt, his grey trousers, his sandals, his nails, his smell gave him away?

A drop of sweat formed in his armpit. He felt it coalesce. Soon it would fall, making him shudder. What would change between now and then? The men would start filing past him, perhaps.

Outside, a truck stood ready to take the chosen ones away. The ones that he and four other hooded men like him would point to.

How had it come to this?

*

Bukit Panjang Village, 18 August 1941, six months earlier

"Fool," she had said, smiling at him. The moonlight played on her. Her narrow eyes were half-closed, and her smile was tight, as if she was trying not to laugh at him.

He did not mind. It felt nice coming from her. He had stood there for a long time. In the clearing in between the thicket of coconut trees, the scent of Pandan leaves filtered out the smells of Bukit Panjang's farms. He would be tired in the morning, and so would she. But as he stood speechless before Fusang, with the breeze that caressed her naked breasts brushing his eyelids and his lips, he knew he had already realized the meaning of life.

He had waited a long time before she came. He could have waited longer. All night. He leaned against a trunk. He did not want to lie down. He was afraid he might fall asleep.

The half-moon night rang with the drone of insects. He joined his palms and looked at their lines, at the curve that the two arcs at the top made. The Kling who drove the bullock cart had told him that he would be lucky and his wife would be very beautiful, with a crescent like that. What did Fusang see in him? He was not sure. A life of hope, perhaps? A life with a man who could read and write. Even a bit of English.

Something changed in the air, and he knew it must be her. She ran into the clearing, barefoot, hair flowing, just as he had imagined. She stopped before him, panting. Her forehead glistened with a thin film of sweat.

He held her hands. His mouth was dry. "You're here," he said.

She smirked in her way. "You're here," she repeated, mimicking him.

He swallowed, and his throat hurt. He had thought through variants of what he would do. One of them entailed tipping her over and getting on top of her. Another had to do with a poem he had composed, of which he did not remember a word.

She sighed, pulled her hands away and stepped back. There was a fluid movement, something he may even have missed, and then she stood naked to the waist.

Ah Ding stood rooted as he gazed at her breasts. He had known they would be small and would define perfection. The rise and fall of her taut nipples and the fine bumps on her aureoles made this different from a dream. His right hand twitched, but he pulled it back. He wanted to prolong time, as he sometimes did when he read a book.

"Fool," she said again. In the soft light, her dimples blossomed. "Will you not taste them?"

The night song of the insects stopped. The points of her breasts rose towards him.

"If I do, I will take you as well," he said.

She closed her eyes. "Take me," she said. Then she opened her eyes and looked deep into his.

That was the moment of his life when he knew what he wanted. "I will take you after I marry you. Soon."

"Are you sure?" she said.

"Do you know how long I have loved you?" he said.

She covered herself and stood on her toes to kiss him on his left cheek. She blushed as her soft belly rubbed against his erection. She hugged him, giggled, and stepped away. She sat with her back against a trunk. He lay with his head on her lap. The pounding in his chest had stopped, and the song of the insects had returned. Laden with her scent, the breeze slowed down around her. He smelled her womanhood, and when he looked up, he saw her eyes moist with love. Her face was framed by a cloudy but moonlit sky.

"How long?" she said.

"We were very small. You had missing teeth, your gums showed. I was ill, I had a fever. Mother said I couldn't come and play. You came inside and rubbed my head."

She stroked his hair. He liked the soft scratching of her nails on his scalp.

He had been a fool. But it was a time of innocence.

*

Off Bukit Timah Road, Sixth Milestone, 12 February 1942

"Fool," Madam Cheng had said to her husband. "Do it now!" The sound of guns and mortar had faded away, to be replaced by the shrill, faltering hum of the insects.

Madam Cheng sat on the ground, her back against the Seraya tree. Cheng was next to her, quaking. Ah Ding stood there with his back to the two of them. The mixed fragrance of the forest and the soft moonlight reminded him of the time with Fusang.

The night was split wide open by a mortar shell exploding a few hundred metres away. When his hearing returned, he waited for the thudding of Dalforce's Lee Enfield Mark Is. They were few, and when they did speak up, it only meant that more of his Company X were about to fall to the Japanese.

"They are close," Ah Ding said. His voice came out squeaky. This was not how he wanted to talk. He had not eaten in the day. And he had forced Madam Cheng to drink the last drops of water from his canteen. Now the dryness of his tongue and the emptiness of his stomach hurt.

He had been ashamed of what fear did to him. When he told her, Madam Cheng had stroked his head and planted a kiss on it. It had made him tingle and feel warm. It was a long time since his mother had kissed him. "Don't be afraid of fear," she had said, looking serious. Then she chuckled. "The worst it can do, if you are brave enough, is dirty your pants. And that will not matter where we are going." Her face had crinkled into a warm smile. One of her yellow teeth was chipped.

She sat there in the dark. He did not dare to look over his shoulder. Her words came out in a rush. Her voice was dulcet. He could imagine her head tilted to her right, her lips trembling, her eyes blazing.

"You said it first!" she said to Cheng. "You told me you wouldn't let me fall into their hands."

Cheng's wail drowned out the distant sounds of war and the song of the insects. Ah Ding clamped his hands over his ears. A hand clamped his shoulder. It was Cheng.

"You do it," Cheng said. "It has to be done. She is right." His eyes were vacant. "Use your revolver," he said. He pointed to it as if he needed to tell Ah Ding which one to use. He pointed again at it as he stepped past Ah Ding, brushing against him and walking onto the gap in the thicket.

"Ah Ding, Son! Make it quick." Madam Cheng called out. Ah Ding's mind flickered to some distant moment in the Chengs's house when she had said those same words. The scent of tea wafted through from that distant time. "Ah Ding?" Her tone was harsher now.

Ah Ding stepped towards her. He felt her eyes on him and turned his face away.

"What, pants still dry?" She chuckled.

Ah Ding laughed. Then he was on his knees, sobbing, letting her cradle his head against her breast.

"They are all around us," she said. "It is finished. Let Teacher Cheng guide you. He is a good man, you know ... We grew old together, he and I ... but I am not old enough to be safe. You and the others ... you have your lives ahead of you."

He sat with his head between his knees. He fought back the bile. She gripped his arm so tight that it hurt. "Now, Ah Ding, now! Do not think. You think too much. Be a man. Look away from me after you are sure you have pointed right. Do not look at me. Then squeeze. That is all."

He nodded. She held his chin and turned his face so that her eyes bored into him. He lowered his eyes.

His knees screamed as he stood up. The revolver felt cold and heavy. His hands shook. She held his hands in hers to steady them. "Do not look at me," she said.

*

He retched again. His body had only air to expel. There was something vile inside, but it did not leave him. He smelled the grass and the mud, and he wanted them to swallow him up into their warmth. He remembered how it had been in the field off Choa Chu Kang Road. The hundreds of warm, uniformed bodies, the softness of the earth and how his stomach had churned when he understood that it was not water that made the earth soft.

He thought of Madam Cheng in all her dignity. Her single streak of silver hair, cultivated to let young men like him know she was not much younger than her husband, the teacher.

The thought calmed him, and he laid his forehead on the banyan leaf shape that he liked to form with his thumbs and fingers.

A slight pressure nudged his shoulder. It was Cheng. Ah Ding let himself be guided into standing position. He felt nothing. There was a blur, and his cheek stung. It was Cheng slapping him. Then, Cheng clasped Ah Ding's cheeks in both hands and kissed him on the forehead.

Cheng's hands fumbled along Ah Ding's sleeves. Later, Ah Ding realized that was when Cheng had removed his red triangle. Next, Cheng removed the yellow cloth around Ah Ding's head. Ah Ding felt the breeze ruffle his matted hair.

"I'll take this," Cheng said as he patted a bulge in his side. That would be Ah Ding's revolver.

"Now, we part," Cheng spoke again. "I'll go that way." He jerked his thumb backwards. "You …" He pointed his index finger the other way. He gripped Ah Ding's biceps. "Look at me now," he hissed.

Two shots broke out from not too far away. They were Dalforce Lee Enfields. Cheng nodded as if he had known they would sound at that exact moment.

Cheng's eyes were red. He said, "Do not walk along the road. Clear?"

Ah Ding stood still.

"Clear or not?" Cheng shouted.

Ah Ding nodded.

"Go now." It was almost a whisper. There were more gunshots. They were closer.

"Will that be all?" Ah Ding said.

"Yes," Cheng turned around with his rifle slung over his shoulder. When he had taken a few steps, he looked back. Ah Ding had not moved.

"Go! Go now!" Cheng shouted. He came running to Ah Ding, turned him around, and shoved him. Ah Ding walked towards the city.

*

Bukit Panjang Village, 16 February 1942

The sky was grey and patchy. Ah Ding shivered as the water and slush covered his feverish body. He looked at the dark clouds. One night long ago, he had squeezed Fusang's hand, and she had squeezed his. They had sat away from the crowd of men listening to the storyteller performing under the banyan tree. The storyteller's wizened face lit up when he saw the two of them. Other men in the crowd had turned to look at the young couple. Some of them whispered, but mostly they minded their own business. The storyteller told of Yinglong, the dragon, the rain deity, and how with his breath he created clouds of the most intricate shapes. Ah Ding had felt a lightness in his heart as he thought of hugging Fusang. He had imagined clouds shaped like her breasts and buttocks.

One of the clouds in the sky over him now was frothy. A few drops of warm rain swerved as they approached his eyes. One fell on his wet cheek. How he would have liked it to rain harder. He imagined he was pushing himself down into the soft slush where pigs used to laze a few days ago. He imagined the stinky water closing in on him, cocooning him and freeing him. The sky and the clouds would blur and disappear. The mud would swallow him, and he would change body. Would Fusang let him touch her?

A strong pair of hands lifted him up and away from the slush.

He was carried to the side of the fish pond. Through wet eyes, he saw a face that gave him no comfort. It was grim and pockmarked. The man's breath remained steady. He did not speak.

It was the night soil carrier, Yee. From as far back as he could remember, Ah Ding and his group of five had tormented the man who walked with the two pails of shit balanced along a horizontal pole. They had stalked him and baited him. He took it without a murmur. Ah Ding's father had only slapped him once for doing that. He could still feel the sting of that hard slap.

Ah Ding felt hard ground below him. A rough pair of hands stripped him. Then warm water covered him. Two pairs of hands dried him and covered him with sheets of worn cloth. The sheets smelled of oil, but he did not care. The warmth that coursed through him brought him relief.

Once, he had been too sleepy to get up and too cold to sleep. He had lain, shivering. A blanket draped over him had brought him immense peace. Later, he kissed Mother and thanked her. She giggled and told him it was Father who had covered him.

Now the buzzing in his head and the ache in his heart tormented him. He imagined Fusang calling his name, closing her eyes and pretending it was not happening, bleeding, longing for death.

"Her parents tried to hide her," Yee said. "They cut her hair. We heard it worked for some. Not for her." His wife stood behind him. She was bent and old.

A lump formed in Yee's throat. "She has changed body now. Nothing to be done … We waited for a full day and night for her parents and another day for you to recover. Then we burned her. It is the best way. We have her bones."

Ah Ding sat up. He fainted almost immediately.

*

His father came for him. He clasped his hands and bowed to thank Yee. It was two days after the surrender. People had trickled back into the village. There was nothing for them in the city.

The Japanese had come visiting each night. They had got Fusang the first night. Her parents were missing.

*

Ah Ding wore his father's clothes. The trousers were loose and too short. The shirt was about all right. He sat facing his father. They did not speak. His mother had fussed over him.

"There is nothing we can do," she had said. "We live."

His father had shouted at him when he had announced he was leaving to join the Dalforce, the volunteer Chinese army. "Fools!" he had yelled. "They are fools! Listen to the people who know. Listen to Tan Kah Kee, not to that moron teacher of yours! And his abnormal wife!"

A burning sensation lit up in the middle of Ah Ding's eyes. He imagined himself jumping out of his body and striking down his father.

"You will not do anything! Nothing! Look at what happened in Penang! And do you ... you stupid boys—do you not know? How can you not understand? The Japanese will win. You will not stop them. You will create another Nanjing!"

He had turned his back on his father. His friends Chiang and Yeow were waiting for him.

"Old man give you a hard time?" Chiang asked.

"Hmm," Ah Ding had shrugged.

"That's what I expected. What the hell do these old cocks know?" Yeow had said.

Ah Ding had always been comfortable with his father, unlike Chiang and Yeow, who had been contemptuous of theirs. Ah Ding only listened when they vented their venom on their fathers.

Now he sat facing his father. Words did not form. Yee had clasped something into Ah Ding's hands as they were leaving. It was the ten-dollar note, all crumpled and soggy. But not torn. Ah Ding opened his palm and straightened it out. The face of the British King stared out of it. Chiang had told him that it was special. You could move it all around, from one corner of your eye to another, and the King would still look at you and through you, with his serene half-smile.

His hands trembled as he tried to smooth out the folds and pits in the note. When they had assembled for the last time at HQ on Kim Yam Road, Ah Ding had still not imagined the possibility of this moment. The note had just one fold. It had a fresh scent. Now it smelled of fetid water.

"This ... Shall I give this to Mother?" Ah Ding croaked.

His father's eyes were dull. "It's useless," he said.

"Father?"

"That note. It is not money anymore. The Japanese will have their own money."

Ah Ding turned the note over to the side, where it had many coats of arms. Then he flipped it again, to the side that had the benign monarch and the words "Ten Dollars".

"Don't think too much," his father said. "Ah Ding?" He leaned forward.

Ah Ding saw his father's lips were pursed and his forehead lined. He felt deep exhaustion closing in on him.

The words blaring across the air jolted him. His mother came running into the room.

"All Chinese men", "eighteen to fifty", "Telok Kurau school". They made out some of the phrases.

"It's a loudspeaker," his father said.

*

Bukit Timah Road Checkpoint and Kempeitai East District Branch, 18 February 1942

This earth has a different smell when it is clean. A scent that words do not describe. He would have thought that it was brown, this earth that he took for granted, this soil that they had sworn would never be defiled by the scum from Japan.

Only from this close, he saw grains of earth and a mesh of grass. It was a rusty colour, in fact—a kind of red. It was damp, though the last shower had fizzled out a long time back.

It took some time—he did not know how much—for his eyes to clear and for the grains of soil to come into focus. Now a splotch disturbed their regular pattern. And then another. A spirit stepped out of him and knelt beside him, explaining things, gently pointing them out. "This is your drool. That is your blood," the spirit said. "That is strange," he said to the spirit. "I feel nothing," he said. "No pain, no fear, no anger. Nothing." Without thinking, he straightened up. Now his cheek and his gut, where he had received the slap and the punch, exploded in pain.

The sentry's rifle swung up. Ah Ding knew the make. Arisaka Type 30. The sentry's gaunt face was contorted, his eyes bulging, his nostrils flared. Ah Ding saw a single strand of hair jutting out of the man's nose. The rifle butt had reached its zenith.

The sentry froze. He tottered a bit, lowered his rifle by his side and stood at attention.

Ah Ding felt a nudge in his side and looked over his shoulder. A black open-top car straddled the road. Its nether regions were caked with mud. The upper parts glistened, an imposing mix of glossy black and shining steel.

He fought off a swooning sensation. It was a man who had prodded him. The man's cap hid half of his face. "Coming to the city?" he asked Ah Ding. His voice was soft. He spoke in Hokkien.

Ah Ding's throat hurt. He couldn't open his mouth.

"Know who that is?" The man jerked his thumb at the car that stood behind him, its engine giving off a steady, low rumble.

Ah Ding shook his head.

"You could be dead," the man said. "That's what you boys wanted, yes? To become martyrs?"

A tremor shook the ground as if a mortar had exploded close by without a sound.

*

A gentle breeze fanned him. The creak of a ceiling fan and the whirr of its blades made a comforting rhythm. It reminded him of the fan in Master Cheng's room.

"Ah, you're up. Good, good." It was the man who had spoken to him at the guard post where the sentry had thrashed him. Ah Ding had bowed before the guard—but not low enough.

Ah Ding stood up and felt the ground swivel again. This time, he stayed on his feet. The man patted his hand. He looked at Ah Ding and said, "You are a man. We need you." He nodded for emphasis and stepped back. Ah Ding saw an officer flanked by two adjutants. The officer sat at ease, his right leg crossed over the left.

The room was cool and dank. In spite of the fan, there was a harshness in the air. A light bulb and a lamp at the table exuded a combined brilliance that hurt his eyes. He had never seen so much light inside a room.

The officer took off his peaked cap and flicked it on to his desk. He was almost bald. Ah Ding took in the perfect creases of his uniform, the shiny patches. It was a while before he realized he was being spoken to, and the man who had addressed him earlier was translating.

"My name is Oishi. Colonel Oishi," the officer was saying. "I will not talk much to you. But think about what I have to say.

"Do you know that the war was forced on us? We had no choice?"

He paused, and his mild brown eyes peered through his round glasses, deep into Ah Ding's. "No, I thought not."

He picked a packet of cigarettes from his table and toyed with it. Ah Ding thought he saw the interpreter's eyes flicker. The brown packet had a floral pattern on it. Later, he would know it was called Kinshi.

"Look at you, and look at me. We are one! We are not here to make slaves of you. The white man did that. Do you know what happened at Penang and so many places as they turned and ran from us? Turned and ran like cowards, every one of them!

"Unfortunately … You may know of some bad things that our soldiers …" Oishi's voice trailed off, and the translator bent forward, his hands clasped before him as if leaning would help him catch the words faster.

"General Yamashita's orders were clear. No looting, no arson, no rape. We are executing many soldiers. Do you know that?"

Ah Ding's eyes smarted. Oishi looked at him and lowered his head. He took off his spectacles and inspected them. His forehead was furrowed. "In war, bad things happen. We did not start this war. We cannot control all of it. What happened is behind us. The men you followed were fools. They were fools to provoke us, fools to resist, and they fought like fools. Now we need good men to create a new tomorrow. Syonan will be the new name of this city, and it will—" A phone rang, and an orderly came running into the room. He saluted the Colonel and said something in a guttural tone. Oishi nodded and flicked his hand. The man bowed and ran out.

"Now, now …" The translator faithfully caught every word. "Now we need men like you," Oishi said. "Men like you and Ikeda here. Ikeda will teach you our language. You will see, we will build schools. Hospitals. Make you safe. But first—we must root out all hostiles. We will do a proper screening. How? You. People like you must help us move forward. You yourself—you were a volunteer. I know that. I saw you get up after being hit. And by the way, learn to bow properly. This will no longer be a savage country. Anyway, Ikeda will show you around. You can work with us. If you like."

*

Telok Kurau School Screening Camp, 18 February 1942

"Here. Wear this," Ikeda had said. "Let me check ... yes. You will be fine. Come back straight here. I will tell you what to do. There will be four more like you. We have chosen the best." Ikeda had taken to smiling at Ah Ding. He had an unctuous barber's smile. When he smiled, Ah Ding remembered the scenes of the YMCA building. After he had seen many worse things, it was when he saw fingers being broken that he had fainted again. They had not had to lay a hand on him.

Ah Ding had looked outside the van's window, and his heart had thudded. They sat in rows, hundreds of Chinese men squatting, their eyes lowered. The compound was full of them, but they kept coming in and finding room. He closed his eyes for a moment, and a grating mix of sounds deafened him—treads of boots, barked orders, shuffling of feet, truck engines. He shuddered and opened his eyes.

Ah Ding looked at the black hood. A fly buzzed near his ear. His throat hurt. He put the hood on. He felt light-headed as a silence cocooned him from the commotion outside. The two slits for his eyes were perfectly placed. He would have liked the slits to be smaller. The world looked clearer through them. From a dark recess in his mind, a memory lurched out. On a hot afternoon, Father was sleeping with his specs next to him. Ah Ding had put them on, and the world had dissolved into a blur.

Something was moving. It was Ikeda calling him out with a motion of his finger. He stepped out of the van. The contact of the road with his feet was jarring through the shoes that Ikeda had given him. He had been sitting for too long.

He hoped the ground would sway like it had done earlier, that he would crash out of this intersection of place and time and land somewhere else. He stood there, and the drop of sweat that had been forming dropped down his armpit. He looked at the rows of squatting men. There was Yeow. He was thin and gaunt. He sat on his haunches, head lowered. Not much of a soldier now. Many places away from him was another man that he faintly remembered, one of the rival Guomindang side.

He wanted it to finish soon. The sun was too bright, too hard.

PART 2

7

In Which Siew Chin Looks Into a Mirror

2005, Siew Chin

THERE WAS NOTHING WRONG with the old mirror. I just felt like buying a new one. It's not as if what I see is that different. Since that meeting with the tissue seller—in all these years, I never knew his name—I've been looking, though. Looking at myself more often, for longer.

All the facials and the whitening creams don't matter anymore. I still get the facials, but I stopped the creams a long time back. I can still walk and take a bus on my own, though I don't go out without Michelle by my side. That's not bad for a woman who's been eighty for a while.

I look at the mirror, and it tells me that death is not far away, considering that the days go slow, but the years fly by.

The tissue seller reminded me of how long I have lived. I stand in this scented bathroom, in this enormous flat, in this condo landscaped with Tembusu and Angsana trees. How far away from me is he? It is a small city. He can't be too far away.

How long ago was it when Tiong pulled a chain to show me the working of a flush, that magical invention, that milestone in our journey together? That year was 1962, when we left the shophouse to move into an HDB flat.

And after he left me, Zhu Hua and her mother kept pestering me to move into a condo. Oh yes, I can blame it on them, but I wanted it as well. I can say it now. I shifted here in 1982. Honestly, once I had decided to go on with life—it helped that the business needed me—I did like life's good things. The costly bags, which came into the scene only in the nineteen-eighties, as far as I know, the best hairdressers, the best lingerie. And of course, the best cosmetics.

I even use Japanese brands. I just got talked into it. I wonder what Tiong would have said to that. He was very clear—never a Japanese product, however cheap it was. He left too early, of course, much before they became posh. In his day, they called Japanese cars biscuit tins. He had his Ford Cortina.

Anyway, I stand there, thinking about all this. Michelle comes into the frame. She's checking that I'm okay. She's wearing a red T-shirt and tight white shorts. Tomorrow is Sunday, her day off. She'll be one of the thousand maids around Lucky Plaza. Filipino maids on Orchard Road and Indian workers in Little India. It takes an army to keep people like me living well. I'm removing my make-up with a Shu Uemura cleanser. I dab more of it on the cotton wipe. I like how it cools my skin.

The Straits Times has big articles about new casinos and the jobs they will bring to Singapore. I talked to Lee Ping, the last of my friends whom I call up once in a while. She said, why not go for prostitution if that's the logic?

I don't think she knows about before 1945. I think only Tiong knew, and he kept that secret well. I told her that they already have prostitution. There are ads for escort services in the *Yellow Pages*, and there's nothing wrong with that except that it doesn't generate that much employment. I wasn't joking, but she laughed.

Sometimes I worry that I will end up talking about those three bad years, at the rate at which I'm losing my grip. But it has been sixty years, and I've done my running. I'm done with that now.

Or am I? Meeting that man, the tissue seller, has loosened the lid on some thoughts. What if it comes out, about my bad years, about what they made women like me do? Surely Lee Ping would still be a friend? I used to read every bit I could about the South Koreans, how they stood up and talked about it. Here there has only been silence. Are sixty years of silence enough to smother the screams of the bad times? My forehead has puckered. I shake my head at myself and the creases melt away, leaving behind plain skin. My forehead still looks good. It's the sunken cheeks that I wish I could do something about. I wipe a spot off the mirror with my finger. Ten years ago, even five, I would have given Michelle a scolding for that.

Life could have taken so many paths. I am lucky to stand here now. I sleep well most nights. Last night, I did wake up breathless. It must have had something to do with meeting the tissue seller. But now that I have faced myself, I have had this calming moment, I think I will get over it. No, I'm not too worried about myself. Worrying didn't get me here.

I worry about that man, the tissue seller, though. This is no country for poor people. I have heard about the dead who are only noticed when their stink calls for attention. I often thought about him. I wondered if his enemies finally got him. Apparently not. What brought him to this state, though? He must have no one to look after him. Does he live alone now, this man with his kind eyes who saved me? Tiong and Lai did as well, of course. But they would not have mattered if it wasn't for that man. Tiong came into my life last. He tumbled into my life and stumbled out of it.

What have I done to deserve such guardian angels? But, on the other hand, nothing I did, in any birth, could explain the things men did to me in my bad times.

"Ma'am, are you all right?" Michelle's head is almost perpendicular to the door frame, her black eyes dancing, her lips pressed to show she is holding back a laugh. I should be grateful to her for checking on me. I have stood too long. My ankles hurt.

I would like to smile back at her, to treat her like a close friend. But I keep my distance. "I'm done," I say. "Go to sleep. Good night."

"Good night, Ma'am," she chimes.

I don't ask her to give me a foot bath. I want to be alone. The Teochew porridge was gentle on my stomach, but I still feel uneasy when I slip below the quilt. I change over to the other side of the king bed. It does not help.

Tiong is peering at me from the faded wedding photo. If he was still with me, what would I tell him about the tissue seller? Everything, I think. There was never a reason to hold back anything from Tiong. It's been many days. Years, perhaps? I have not ached for him like this. How silly he was to go like that.

8

Have We Met Before?

1972, Siew Chin

"GIRL OR BOY, TWO IS ENOUGH," the advertisement in *The Straits Times* announced as if that message needed repeating. I folded the crinkled aluminium foil into a layered rectangle as the last bite of the ham sandwich melted away in my mouth. When I was younger, I would sometimes eat two of them. Only after we started doing well, of course. I had nibbled at the edges of the vanilla ice cream ball in the banana split while I ate the sandwich. I like my ice cream a bit mushy, even now, at eighty—what is it, eighty-three? And then, I was … that was 1972.

The gleaming Formica seats and tabletops of the Magnolia Snack Bar, the one on Orchard Road, are so familiar, even though that was the last day I went there. I can still feel the cold of the tabletop on my hands and the smooth, hard, but comfortable seat, usually warmed by the customer who had just left, on my buttocks. The din of the road invaded the place when the door was opened and receded into a hum when it was shut.

A thin plume of smoke rose from behind the newspaper. I heaped bits of vanilla, chocolate and strawberry ice cream and licked the spoon clean. I closed my eyes, and the taste became more intense. Then, as now, a good dessert always made my head tingle.

We've become more sophisticated now. Zhu Hua often takes me to places where they have tiramisu and crème brûlée, and you think nothing of paying ten dollars for their very restrained sweetness. Our pleasures were simpler and cheaper then.

I sensed Tiong looking at me. I opened my eyes to look into his. He let out a tiny, lazy wisp of smoke away from me. He was exceptionally polite in that way. When he smoked in a closed space, he would make sure he didn't exhale big clouds. He lightly rolled the tip of the cigarette against the ashtray. It was his special way, instead of just flicking or tapping the cigarette.

I gobbled up another big chunk and rolled it in my mouth. His eyes had an amused look.

"What?" I said.

"I've finished the paper," he said. He had wolfed down his sandwich, as usual. We had alighted at Specialist Shopping Centre and walked over here. He always picked up a newspaper at the Mamak stall and made a point of reading it while I did justice to my sandwich and ice cream.

"What's new?" I asked.

"Hmm, nothing much," he said.

"What a waste of time, then," I said.

"It's all right." He let out a little smoke. He smiled. I felt like reaching out over the table and caressing his head. The bright afternoon sunlight, filtered by the curtain, played on the side of his face. "They're going to make some kind of island resort on Blakang Mati. They'll call it Sentosa. Someone just won a prize for suggesting that name."

"Sen-toh-saa," I said for the first time.

"Sounds like a stupid name to me, and a stupid idea. They say the name is from santosha, an Indian word. At least they made it easier."

"Who knows?" I said. "It might work. We've been wrong before. Look at us sitting here and eating after watching a movie. People have to have fun, as well. Good clean fun."

"You're eating," he said. "I'm looking at you." He raised his eyebrows and tilted his head.

I licked my lips. "I'll live longer. If there's one good thing I've picked up from my bastard parents, it's that we've got to eat and breathe slower to live longer."

He frowned. "Don't say that. I keep telling you."

"What?" I knew what he meant.

"Don't abuse them. Shut it away, all of it," he said.

I reached out and clasped his hand. "I don't want to live longer," I said.

"Don't get all teary on me," he said. I fought back my tears. "What are you trying? Your bloody nails!" He swatted away my hands.

"I'm sorry," I said when I could speak without choking. I smiled at him to show him I was in control. "I didn't realize ..." I stroked his shoulder. His shirt was cotton. I had bought it at John Little a couple of days before. "I just—I actually don't want to live longer."

He grimaced. "You women." He shook his head as he blew a thin, wispy trail of smoke. "What did you like most in the movie?" We had seen *The Godfather* at Lido.

"Nothing much. Maybe when the old man mourns for his older son. Like I said, it was too violent for me. You?"

He broke into a grin, and I knew what he was going to say. "The breasts. I didn't think, you know, like—tan dhan!" He looked like a pleased schoolboy.

"Of course," I said. I nodded slowly as I attacked the ice cream, making clanking noises with my spoon and getting successively smaller portions. "I didn't see what the fuss was about, anyway."

"Ah, it's just another movie. Next year there will be another bigger one. Can I?" He made the sign for the bill.

"Wah! Let me finish!" I said. He sighed.

*

We got a taxi right away. Tiong raised an imperious hand, and a sleek light-blue NTUC-Comfort screeched to a halt before us. I had told him not to hold the door for me, but he still did it on those rare days when we took taxis. That was one of those days, a lazy weekday when Tiong had had the Cortina picked up to be serviced, and we had gone out for a movie. Life was already quite good for us back then, a far cry from the times when we had started out on the beehoon business.

"Want to read?" he asked, holding the paper out for me.

I took it and eased myself onto the seat. Tiong walked around and got in on the other side. "Queenstown, 50 Stirling Road," he told the driver, who reset the meter. Pirate taxis had vanished from the roads of Singapore only a few years before.

The taxi zoomed off, pinning us to the backs of our seats.

"Not so fast, Brother," Tiong said. He was affable, as always, but he raised his voice just a bit. The driver slowed down.

"I'm not so young anymore," Tiong said, just to assuage the man.

"Oh, not me, boss," the driver said with a laugh. "You want slow; I drive slow. No problem."

Tiong looked ready to light up another of his Navy Cut cigarettes. His hand had wandered to his shirt pocket, lazily pulled out the packet, and he was about to knock it at the bottom to get one of them to pop out. I tapped him on the shoulder and wagged a finger. He rolled his eyes with exaggerated effect and patted the pack back into his pocket. I don't think we ever kissed in public. I was tempted to do it that one time. I imagined leaning forward, feeling his rough cheek on my lips, smelling his Old Spice aftershave.

"I drive safe, Boss," the driver continued breezily. "Though with the right car, not this one, of course, I could do the Grand Prix."

Tiong chuckled. "It's a pity about the boy who died this year, though," he said.

"Yes, Lionel Chan, that's a shame. Young guy," the taxi driver said. "It's that stretch, the Devils' Bend, that's very dangerous. They even say they may cancel the Grand Prix soon."

"Really, no more Grand Prix here?" Tiong craned to catch the driver's eyes in the rear-view mirror.

My attention wandered to the newspaper article about the new resort. A lot had happened in the last few years, and Tiong and I had been lucky. We had worked hard, of course, as he said. I always reminded him that we had worked hard, and there were many others who had worked harder than us. Fifteen years ago, I would have had the *Nanyang Siang Pau* in my hand, not *The Straits Times*. And I would have been stirring beehoon in a big pan, sweating, standing on tired feet.

Those were good years, I thought, and Tiong and the driver pattered on. I had no complaints even then. But I had taken to the easy life quite well. I looked at the advertisement in the bottom right corner. "Girl or Boy, Two Is Enough." It had the familiar picture of two girls under an umbrella, smiling and sharing an apple. It was one of the mysteries of life that Tiong had stayed with me although I couldn't give him children.

He was deep in conversation with the driver. I had switched off from listening to them. Tiong turned to me, puzzled. I guessed that I had squeezed his hand. I shook my head to tell him it was nothing.

He frowned and returned to his conversation. "You know," he said, "We've met before. I'm very good with faces, but surprisingly, I can't quite locate yours."

The driver was silent for a while. Then he said, "Many passengers tell me that. I think I have a common face."

I folded the newspaper into my handbag. We had just sped by Princess House. We would be home soon.

"What do you think of the airline? Will it survive?" Tiong asked the driver. I knew what he was up to. He was a firm believer in the wisdom of taxi drivers. Quite often, he asked them about their favourite eating places and about the restaurants and shops we supplied.

The driver was silent. Tiong bent and inclined his head to catch the man's eye. The driver had stiffened a bit. When he spoke, he seemed to have lost his enthusiasm for the conversation.

"Hard to say, Boss. They changed the name already, what? From Mercury Singapore Airlines to Singapore Airlines. Just because the other side complained, the Malaysians. Should have guts. How can they survive without guts?"

"True," Tiong said. "First thing is to have guts."

We were on Commonwealth Avenue already. I let out a big yawn, covering my mouth with the back of my hand. It would be nice to nap for a bit. There was plenty of time to work out the supplies for the next few days and talk to the factory manager.

"Where have we met before, though?" Tiong said. He had that frown that told me he was irritated with himself at letting something slip. He was very good with faces and names.

The taxi lurched a bit as the driver's foot squeezed the accelerator. He did not say anything.

"You have no idea?" Tiong persisted with a puzzled smile.

The driver made a show of looking all around as he navigated a left turn. He took his time before he replied. "No, boss." Something in the way he said it suggested that he was done with talking. We were almost there, anyway. He was a strange man, this taxi driver, I remember thinking, to rebuff someone as amiable as Tiong.

When we got off, Tiong rounded up the fare, eighty-five cents, to a dollar. As I stepped out, I heard the driver mutter a reluctant thank you. Tiong shut his door a bit louder than he needed to. The taxi roared off.

Tiong followed it with his eyes for a while. "Strange man," he muttered.

I slipped my arm into his. Two girls in school uniforms walked by. There were Queenstown Secondary School girls. It was only a year since the school had opened to girls. One of the two blushed as she saw me snuggle up to Tiong.

"You can close your eyes and imagine it's that woman," I told him.

"What woman?" he said.

"Fool. The one whose breasts are all you remember from the film. Her name is Simonetta Stefanelli, by the way."

He could have said that I was too flat-chested, but he wasn't the type. His eyes crinkled, and he grinned at me.

I was forty-nine, and we had been together for twenty-seven years. That was the only time I kind of asked him to make love to me.

"I don't need to think of anyone," he said.

"I don't know what you see in me," I said.

"You look like you're about to cry."

"Don't be silly." My skin was tingling all over.

We walked faster towards the lift. We were on the seventh floor. The lift stopped on odd floors. Inside the lift, I pulled him to me. He squeezed me against his chest and kissed me on the forehead. I shivered.

He yanked the grill open, and we stepped out, almost running, still holding hands. Then he stopped without warning. He used his other hand to steady me as I nearly tripped.

"What's wrong?" I asked him. His eyes were wide, and his mouth was open.

He let out a long breath and leaned against the railing. Our flat was at the far end of the corridor. He was breathing heavily. He looked like he could collapse any time.

"What is it, Tiong?" I nearly shouted. Behind me, the door to a flat was open, and only the grill gate was bolted. That was a common practice to keep air circulating in those flats. I heard padded footsteps as someone approached the gate to check what the noise was about.

Tiong lowered his head. He held my hands tight. He looked over his shoulder at the path the taxi had taken.

"Let's go," he said.

I opened the lock after fumbling for the key, which had slipped deep into my handbag. Tiong let me guide him to the rexine-covered sofa. As soon as he had sat down, I ran to get him a glass of water.

He waved it away and motioned for me to sit next to him. He was shaking his head in the peculiar way that he had. It meant that he was talking to himself in his mind. Then he turned to me. "I have to settle a score," he said.

I stroked his hair. It was short and very soft. I pressed down gently on his head to make him rest it on the arc of my shoulder and breast.

He pulled back. He sat slumped for some time, his eyes unfocused. Then he straightened up and looked into my eyes.

"There are things that happened in … in 1942 that I had forgotten. What happened to you was bad. I also went through a bad time.

"When I told you, again and again, to wall up what happened before 1945, I did it because I knew I had to do exactly that to survive as well. The past is a swamp, and if we don't stay away from it, it will suck us in and snuff us out."

He looked at the scarred palm of his right hand.

"Tell me what is going on, Tiong," I said. "I told you some things about the comfort station. I didn't hide much from you. And because you heard me and accepted me, I have this life. But you never told me you needed to wipe a slate clean as well."

He shook his head. "It's that man, the taxi driver. I'm sure of it. He almost got me killed."

"Is that why you told him …? But how can you be sure? Think about it, Tiong. It's, what, thirty or more years ago."

"It's his eyes. A cut in the eyebrow and their shape. I know it was him. And, by God, I'll track him down and get him."

"I'll help you," I said. "Tell me how."

His eyes glazed again. "No, this I have to do myself, just as you exorcised your ghosts yourself."

"You helped me, Tiong."

"Not much. I'll do this alone."

Those would be his last coherent words for a while, till he told me his story from his deathbed.

*

His descent into madness was rapid. That afternoon, he called NTUC-Comfort first and harangued the operator for not being able to locate the driver from the details he gave. Almost as soon as he had finished, he shot out of the house, giving me a squeeze on my shoulder.

It hurt me that he did not let me become his partner in his search, in whatever crackpot scheme he had in mind. When I looked back later, I understood that he was trying to shield me from digging up memories that I buried under the debris of time, memories of being roughly used by fifty men a day for three years.

What can I say about my inability to help him, as he had helped me back in 1945? If I have to explain myself, if there is such a thing as a reckoning, I will say that when Tiong came back home that night, he was already lost because he had become a different man.

He was drunk. He rang the bell at eleven and lurched in, avoiding my eyes. When he bent to take off his shoes, he stayed bent for a while before vomiting on the floor.

I helped him up and steered him to the bathroom, where he vomited another time, this time into the commode. He let me help him up, wash his face, and undress and wipe him. After he collapsed into bed, I cleaned up the mess in the drawing room.

I sat beside him as he lay flat on his back. I stroked his hair and placed his hand on my breast. I looked at his deformed palm and asked Kwan Im to forgive me for not piercing the wall he had built around his life during the war and the occupation. I had to wall off those years to live. That was what Tiong told me to do, and he was right. But perhaps we should have talked about his memories, about things that had happened, that singed the lines of his palm. I cried because I suspected it was too late then.

I was woken up by the phone ringing. The call came from the factory. It was the manager, Boey. He had been waiting for Tiong to tell him what to do about an order from a restaurant in Bukit Timah. They wanted to buy on credit. Tiong had been against the idea, but I had convinced him that we should go eat at the place. If the food and the service were good, they would be good people to do business with. I told the manager what I had decided. There would be credit, but with limits of time and value. And we would be exclusive suppliers. I told him the night shift could go ahead. He asked to speak to Tiong, and I told him that was not needed. When I placed the receiver on the hook—it was a new sleek grey phone that we had got to replace the big black one—I had become the head of People's Beehoon Factory.

*

"How can you take it? How long has this gone on?" Lee Ping was always very poised, very much in control. She was petite and slim. We had met through our husbands, but now we met more often than they did.

"Let me get a cup of tea," I said.

"No, Siew Chin, stay here," she said. She sat erect, her hands placed tidily in her lap. I often wondered how it was between her and her husband in bed. Was she the tiger woman there as well?

"I've asked you a few times by now, Siew Chin, and I've never got a good reply. How can you let him do this? Remember the last time, what was it, five years ago?"

"What happened five years ago?" I asked.

"Oh, for God's sake, he was so drunk, he ended up in Hill Street Police Station. Do you really not remember?"

"Ah, that. That was nothing. I'm worried about this time. It's been two days already."

"And the way he bossed you around when we visited the factory. Don't tell me you don't remember that either."

I sighed. "He's a regular man in some ways. He had to show his workers who was the boss. By then, I had already turned out to be right and proven him wrong a few times. That was okay, the way he acted in the factory."

"Why do you take it? That's what I'm asking you."

"Don't be a fool," I said. "I take it because he is a good man, and— well, he loves me. I can be sure he doesn't chase other women." I stopped to let that sink in. Her eyes breathed fire. "I have to have tea. I've got a new one from Pek Sin Choon, Golden Cassia." I beat a retreat into the kitchen. She followed me.

"You're not getting away from me," she said. But she was smiling now. "You have to put your foot down."

"Help me," I said. "Talk to him. He's gone crazy after … well, we took a taxi ride, and he thinks the taxi driver was someone he crossed paths with in 1942. Crossed paths in the wrong way. He's got something to avenge. So he's been out on the streets, visiting the NTUC-Comfort office, talking to a detective, trying to talk to friends in the police. Nothing works. It could have been someone who borrowed the taxi. We didn't ask for a receipt."

"And drinking will make it work?"

"Why don't you wait till he's back and try talking sense into him? You know he's terrified of you. He's always said you're a mulaohu, a tigress. Oh, I don't disagree." The water had boiled. I turned off the gas and poured the water into the pot. I picked up the tray, and we went back into the drawing-room. I put the tray on the centre table and motioned for Lee Ping to wait. I went to our bedroom to check on Tiong. He lay sprawled on the bed, arms and legs pointing in different directions.

"What does he want?" Lee Ping said. She had followed me.

I shut the door on him and went back to the sofa. Lee Ping poured the tea for both of us. She raised her cup and inhaled its vapour, her eyes closed. "It's wonderful."

"Take some," I said. "I have a lot."

"Don't be silly. I'll buy it. Tell me, what does he want? To trace that taxi driver down? And what will he do after that?"

"What he will do, I don't know. What is there to do now?"

"Do you know what it is about? What happened between them?"

"No. Tiong just won't talk about that part of his life."

"I've seen the scar on his hand and wondered how he got it. Do you really not know?"

I shrugged. "No, really." That Tiong chose not to talk about those years to make sure he helped me erase them was not something I could tell her, however close we became. I did come close to telling her then, but I held back.

What made me hold back? Even today, I don't believe I can talk about that part of my past. At Haw Par Villa, in the Second Court of Hell, Yama throws prostitutes into a pool of blood to drown them. There is no punishment for their pimps or their customers. LKY said that comfort stations saved the purity of Singaporean women. I think about talking about those times, but my guess is that I will let my secret fester inside me till they burn my body and I reach the First Court of Hell.

She snapped her fingers. "What are you thinking now?"

I thought: If I told you that I was a comfort woman for three years, would you still come back? Sit next to me? I said, "Nothing much."

"What a mannish reply. Look, I know you're both romantic lover types, but you're too docile, you let him dominate you too much."

I gave her a hard look.

"Ooh, now look who's become a tigress," she shrank back in mock fear. "But tell me, you used to have those fits of anger, you can stare down the workers at the factory, negotiate with customers. What does your man do that reduces you to jelly?"

"He does a few things right."

She burst into a throaty laugh.

"It's not sex," I said. "He gave me this life. He helped me get over those periods of anger and depression. He smoothed out problems I created in my younger days, when I couldn't control my anger. He's done more for me than most husbands do for their wives. Including yours." I smiled without malice. "It matters because I'm an orphan."

"Hmm. Why don't you tell him you'll go with him? What does he do anyway, prowl the streets looking for that taxi driver?"

"I don't know. He just won't take me. And the business has to be kept running."

"Should he see a, you know, someone?"

"A mental health doctor? Oh, I don't see him agreeing to that."

She reached out and squeezed my hand. "I wish there was something I could do."

"I hope he'll get over it," I said.

*

He didn't.

I was curled up on the sofa, waiting for Tiong to stagger back home. I had kept the door open and the gate locked, so that I could see him as soon as he got home. Lee Ping had given me her copy of *If We Dream Too Long*. It was unsettling and depressing, but I liked it that I could read in English, thanks to Tiong. I would pick up a Barbara Cartland or something like that next.

I had almost drifted off into sleep a few times. When the phone rang, it startled me. I put the book aside, careful to leave it open at the page I was on, took off my reading glasses and ran for the phone. I remember thinking, "Oh no, it's the police station again."

"Is that the wife of Mr Lim Tiong?" a woman asked.

"Yes, I am Lim Siew Chin," I said.

"I'm calling from General Hospital."

*

My eyelids were heavy and my throat was parched. I tried to slide back into sleep, but it was no use. Someone was shaking me, and my shoulder hurt from that person's grip.

It was a dark-skinned nurse in a brilliant white uniform. Her forehead was furrowed with lines that disappeared as she saw that I had woken up. She smiled and said, "He has opened his eyes, and he's asking for you."

My back ached and my vision was blurred. It took me a while to place myself. I was sitting by the bed in Bowyer Ward.

"Are you all right?" the nurse asked as I struggled to my feet.

I nodded to thank her. I had been quite calm all along. The taxi driver knew the Chinese name for the hospital, Si-Pai-Po. He had turned around to say some words of encouragement when he returned my change. His words didn't register, but I had mumbled my thanks.

I had fought back my tears as I saw Tiong lying prone, his face purple, a thick bandage around his head, the bottle of dark, almost black blood being dripped into his body.

Now he was awake and looking at me. His lips moved.

"Talk to him," the nurse said.

I wiped off my tears with the sleeve of my shirt. Tiong's hand twitched. He was trying to raise it towards me. I took it and bent to press my cheek against it. I kissed his hand and his forehead.

"My lifeline," he said. His words were clear, just very soft.

"You will get well, Tiong," I said. "You won't leave me, will you?" The shadow of a smile that had lit his face disappeared. "I'm going, Siew Chin," he said.

Later they told me he had crashed the car into a street light at high speed.

He clutched my hand. He said, "Promise me something."

I nodded and kissed his forehead again. "Yes," I said.

"Be strong. And just remember to forget the bad years. So much good happened later. Just erase the bad. I did. But then I went crazy after that man, that taxi driver. It wasn't worth this."

I sat by his side and stroked his cheeks.

"I'll tell you what happened to me. Just don't be a fool like me, even when I'm not around for you. Move forward. Don't use the reverse gear."

The lump in my throat made it impossible for me to speak.

He stayed lucid for a long time. In his soft, clear voice, he told me most of the story that remains etched in my mind. He told it to me in much more detail than I had ever told him about the horrors I had gone through. I kept my promise to him. I moved on with life. I did not need love, physical or emotional, from another man because he gave me enough for this life.

Did I embellish his story? I think he told it in a way that made me fill in some details. But first, let me tell you the story of how we met and fell in love.

9

What Is Love?

1945, Siew Chin

I PICKED UP THE YELLOW Knife tin and tipped oil into the wok. The tin was three-fourths full, and its hook cut into the flesh of my bony fingers. The charcoal gave off its steady heat. When the first fumes of vapour rose lazily from the oil, I toppled the chopped onions into it. My eyes smarted, but I hummed a tune as the onion sizzled and gave off a scent that I had not smelled for three years.

Since Lai had let me take over the cooking and most of the running of the stall, she had more time to negotiate with the suppliers. Under the Ang Mohs, there was more to be had if you had the money to bribe them, and it was getting better day by day. From tapioca and sweet potatoes, we diversified to onions, cabbages, carrots and even bean sprouts. It was not impossible to get eggs. For those who cooked meat, there was even chicken to be had. The prices were ridiculous, of course, and many customers still went for the basic fried beehoon with tapioca. There were more customers each day.

Lai had told me of the hardships of the three years, of standing at the stall without having a single customer for long hours. Of people sweeping the streets after the rice truck had passed by.

I wiped the sweat off my forehead with the sleeve of my formless black shirt. My body had become an alien creature, with whims of its own, after the bad years at the comfort station. I rarely felt hunger. But the one sensation that I enjoyed was the warmth and layers of flavour that accumulated as I cooked in the stall. I worked from about ten in the morning to eight at night, with short breaks in between, and there was not much time to brood. There was no question of fearing hunger, even if I had felt it. At the end of every night, there was the certainty that I could get into the corner of the second floor that Lai had set aside for me, draw the curtain and rest my body.

My mind refused to rest. The dreams visited me without fail. I would wake up breathless and rest my back against the wall. The relief would sink in slowly. A voice would remind me that it was all past. Lai had taken me to a doctor at Kandang Kerbau and got me medicine that cured the sickness those animals in the comfort station had pumped into me. The medicine had deadened the burning and the extreme agony. Now there were mild aches and pains that I could live with. It was the dreams that tormented me, the images of contorted faces, heaving shoulders.

In my first week at the stall, I had shouted at a man who had tried to sweet-talk to me, one of those men who look into your eyes as if they can't wait to penetrate you. Lai had gripped my shoulder and told me to shut up. Then she turned to the man and told him he should not have been born. She spoke softly to him. He never came back.

Lai accosted me when I was done cleaning that night. She still wore a red bandana around her head. Her hair was cut short. She told me that if I did that again, if I shouted at a customer, I would be out on the street. Men would want me and ask for me. It was my job to say no.

When I couldn't hold back my tears, her face hardened. She told me it was no use crying.

I told her about my bad years. Her face remained impassive, but she said she had left behind her womanhood to live. She had worked as a labourer, sent money to her family in Fujian, and only started saving for herself after her family was wiped out. She had taken me in because of the man who had sent me and because she could do with help. On the other hand, she could do without help as well. Now that I had told her about my past, I would find it easier to move on. She also had a past she wanted to leave behind in Fujian.

Those few flat, outwardly unkind words and her many acts of kindness—including taking me to the doctors at KK—changed my life.

As I stood there in the stall, inhaling the flavour of sweetening onion, I thanked Kwan Im again, and I did many times each day. It was time to blanch the beehoon and add it to the wok. The springy noodles hissed as they came into contact with the oil. I tipped the sauce onto them and stirred the mixture.

The customer was a fat, well-dressed woman carrying a baby on her hip. She watched every step that I performed. When I scraped every last bit of beehoon onto the big Upeh leaf, I told her it was the first time I cooked with onions. She gave me the money, shiny new coins issued by the Ang Mohs.

The next few customers were men. The day's orders were simple. Big or small, and how many packets. The man who delivered beehoon packets trundled in on his bicycle. That was Tiong. He used to come around noon. For many days, he came and went without talking much to me. He made his deliveries around noon first. His boss had a clear deal with Lai. They would deliver twice a week and generally ensure we had enough stock for an entire week, just in case something went wrong. Tiong would basically replace the boxes we had consumed and collect money every week.

There was something different about Tiong even then. He was thin and wiry, far removed from most women's idea of a handsome man. But he was tall, and he had a certain presence. It meant nothing to me, but I noticed women eyeing him. The one thing I noticed was that he did not have the piercing look that most men do—or maybe it was something I saw in men, a desire to strip and hurt me. The thing about Tiong was that he never really looked straight at me.

That day, like all other days, he just nodded as he left. "I put the boxes," he said.

"Thank you," I said.

This went on for six months. He would tell me how many boxes he had put there. I would say something to acknowledge him. Once I took over the handling of money, I paid him as well. For many weeks, I made it a point to tally what he had reported with what was on the shelves. I noticed that Lai never bothered to check his bills. I stopped checking as well. It was good to be able to count on honesty.

If it had not been for Lai, Kwan Im bless her, I wonder how different things would have turned out. The bastard Japanese had gone, and I enjoyed the sight of the Japanese soldiers taking our shit away for a few weeks. But the bastard Ang Mohs did not make life that much better for us right away. Yes, we could eat a little better bit by bit. Slowly, if you could pay, you got eggs, meat, good Thai rice, vegetables. But my visit to KK reminded me of how much misery there remained in the city.

Things settled into a routine. We had dozens of customers every day. My feet hurt from standing for long hours. A few times when Lai saw me shifting my weight on my feet, she told me, in her gruff, manly way, to sit for a while. She did make it a point not to spoil me. She told me that if I had been a construction worker, I would have known the meaning of hard work. When she took me in on the night of 12 September 1945, after I had knocked on her door, tired, hungry and scared after that long walk and the bus ride, she warned me not to expect mercy. When I thanked her and steeled myself for a harsh life, I did not know how much mercy she would shower on me. She gave me a safe corner to sleep in when I was young, pretty, and alone. She gave me work that made the days pass in a blur. For a week, Lai stood by my side, teaching me the things I needed to do, warding off men who tried to get fresh with me. She made me handle the money, keeping an eye on me for some time and not bothering to hide that she was watching me. Slowly, she let me take on most of the work with the customers. After about a month, she told me to make the payments to Tiong and the other suppliers as well. When I look back now, I appreciate that apart from the priest at the Kwan Im Temple and her friend Boi, who lived with her as a tenant, I was the only one whom she made part of her life.

*

It was six months before Tiong asked me out. He suggested a film at the Pavilion Cinema. The name of the film, *Spellbound*, did not mean anything to me.

"Six boxes," he said as he came out of the room.

I nodded, making a mental note. It had stopped checking a long time back. I could make him out from a distance on the days he came to the shop. There was something about the way he sat, straight-backed, on his black cycle. When he stopped in front of the shop, he would slide down his left foot to the ground and bring his right leg over the handlebar in a fluid motion. There was a large carrier at the back. His hair was neatly parted, and I always had the feeling that he had combed it just before he had reached the shop. I imagined him looking at the mirror on the handlebar, frowning as he ran the comb through his hair.

He looked at me, but there was something in his way of looking that was not threatening. When he talked about supplies or took payments, he did it in a respectful and distant way. His shirts and trousers were always clean. Not spotless, of course, in those days, as they became later. Spotless did not exist in our world in 1945.

The shirt would be white, a proper buttoned shirt, always tucked in. I guessed he only had one pair of trousers, and later I found I was right. He wore leather shoes with dark socks. About a month after I saw him for the first time, I sensed that there was something different about him. It took me a few days to figure out that it was a new belt, which changed his profile in a barely perceptible way. He kept his right palm out of sight as much as he could. It had a scar disfiguring most of it.

When I nodded in response to his count of six boxes, I expected him to keep going, swing his right leg over the handlebar of the cycle, squeeze the red horn and slide the bicycle forward, off its stand. Just before pedalling off in his straight-backed cycling posture, he would turn towards me for a moment. His eyes would barely meet mine. In the sliver of time that our eyes met, I would give him a half-smile. That had become the routine.

That day, he stood at the passage, a few feet away. I finished packing an order for two large packets. The customer was a schoolboy, a regular whose parents sent him over quite often.

When the boy had left, I looked at Tiong. He wore his relaxed smile, but I could tell that it was a bit of an act.

"It's Kwan Im's first birthday in three days," he said.

I did not know what to make of that. Of course, it was. We would get bigger crowds. We were stocking up. It became a bit of a joke between us later, those first words of his to me that had nothing to do with work.

"Do you want to see a film with me? On the Sunday after, when you are closed? I have asked Madam Lai," he said.

I stared at him. "A film?" I said.

"Yes, at Pavilion. They are showing *Spellbound*. A new film, very famous."

I stood silent, keeping a straight face. It was a rare time when there were no customers. Of course, Tiong had been trying to hit upon a time for his visit when the queue was short. Three in the afternoon was good from that point of view.

"You know the Pavilion, right?" he said. "In Orchard. It's air-conditioned."

"I've never been in an air-conditioned place," I said. "The film—it's in English?"

"Yes, it's very famous," he said.

I smiled. "But what's the point? I won't understand it."

"You don't have to understand all the words," he said. "Even I don't. But anyway, I'm learning. We all better learn." He shrugged to show it was well understood.

I must have let my wonder show.

"Well, bit by bit, anyway," he said.

I gave him a smile. "It won't work for me, that film, I think." I pointed to the customers who were approaching, a couple of young priests from the Indian temple.

"I'll be back the day after the birthday," he said. He went without waiting for me to reply. When he got on his cycle, one of the priests was in the way, ordering in Malay. Tiong pedalled off. His bicycle moved faster than usual.

The next time he came, there were a dozen customers. Lai had joined me. She was taking orders and handling the packing and the money. Tiong raised an open left hand to show five boxes, and I smiled back at him.

The next two times, the queues were long, and there was no question of talking about anything other than materials and money. In the meantime, though, Lai had confirmed that she had encouraged Tiong on his heroic path to broadening his conversation with me.

I reflected on where our budding romance could head. When I lay down on the thin mattress and pulled the curtain around me, there were a few moments I had to myself before sleep drowned out the ache in my lower back and the dull pressure of the hard red-oxide painted floor on every point of my body that came in contact with it. I thanked Kwan Im for giving me that secure corner, for freeing me from being pierced by far worse pains. If my family had taken me in, I would have a soft mat under me. The song of the night would have been the melodious hum of crickets. But I would have been spoiled goods for life. There would not have been a visit to the doctor who gave me pills that numbed me and purged the sickness of the comfort station from me. I thought of the unlikely prince on his black cycle who clearly thought he was destined for a better life in which he spoke English.

There was only one conclusion. To hope was to deceive myself. I could deceive Tiong, perhaps, though I did not know what Lai would have to say about that. The truth was, I was lucky to have what I had. I must model my life on Lai's. There was no point in denying my three bad years or in trying to erase them. But I could go on by walling them up, by living in the present. Lai had done that. She was a rape victim. She had settled on a path of a solitary life in a land far away from her village, and she was better off than many women who had men in their lives. She had chosen me to perform her last rites, and I would not let her down.

I stayed awake longer than usual on the night when I reached this conclusion. Lai had fallen into her deep sleep. Her snores were drowned out by Boi, her equally manly friend from her days as a construction worker. Boi used to sleep in a section on the far side. The snores of the two women had settled into an amicable duet. If I lived to be like the two of them, independent and respected, with a place to sleep in and the ability to help other women, I would gladly look forward to growing into an old, toothless woman who wheezed and snored in her sleep.

*

"How about a Chinese one?" Tiong said. He had finally found me alone.

My puzzlement must have shown. He was like that the first few times, nervous and fumbling with his words.

"A movie, I mean," he said. "At the Majestic. There's one called *The Iron Hand*."

It would be in Cantonese, but that was not the point. I had thought it over. I had a new life here. I feared for what would happen when someone from my kampung recognized me. Should I risk it all by telling him?

The words came out easily enough. "The Japanese came to our house in 1942. One of them spoke Hokkien. He said, 'We were told there is a pretty girl here.' They dragged me away in a truck full of other girls. The first day, they took turns. One held my hands first. Later they did not need to. Every day, the men queued up for us. For three years." A red rage came over me as my tears started flowing. I hated myself for crying. I covered myself with the sleeve of my grey blouse. I tried to stop my shoulder from heaving, but it was no use. I was afraid to remove my arm and seized by a strange desire to hit Tiong. My nose was dripping.

A firm hand gripped my shoulder. I removed my arm from my eyes. It was Lai. She showed no emotion. She flicked her hand to signal that I should go to the back, into the store. I ran there.

The floor seemed to swerve. I grabbed the edge of a marble-top table and lowered myself on the stool next to it. When my blurred vision cleared, I saw that Tiong had followed me.

"Lai had told me about it," he said. "She would not have kept it from me. I don't believe in spoiled goods." He turned his right palm to face me. "I have my memories. I have moved on because I was lucky. Let me know about the film, this Sunday or next."

When he returned three days later, there were customers with large orders. The wok was sizzling, and I was drenched in sweat. We had eggs and vegetables quite regularly now, and the flavours that filled the stall were richer and fuller. Tiong signalled how many boxes he had delivered.

The next time, he waited for the customer, an elderly Malay man, to take the order and go.

"Well?" Tiong said.

"I don't think a film will work. I have to understand it." I smiled. "I've never been to Changi beach. Can we go there instead? It will be nice. I can carry food for us. I'll buy it from People's Park."

A flicker in his eyes told me how repulsive he found the idea.

"What?" I said.

"Well, honestly, I like you a lot. But you will have to get used to one thing for sure, and I don't want to discuss it too much—I am not a beach person. Not Changi beach, not Tanah Merah. No beaches." He grinned. "I'll show you other things. Mountains, snow even."

I put my hands on my hips and gave him a knowing look.

"Oh I will. Don't ask me where." As it turned out, we saw a lot of snow. We went to the Riviera as well, twenty years later. "I'm not just talking. Snow is in the future." He had a way of smiling at you with his eyes, and it convinced you of his goodness. As he lost his nervousness with me, he became his natural self and much easier to be with. "Tell you what, I know the place. Bedok Rest House. You don't need to cook. Yes, Bedok Rest House is the place."

"What is that?" I said.

"It is a great place for seafood. Have you had any recently?"

I looked askance at him.

"Good, then. We'll go by trolley bus to Joo Chiat and change from there."

"Won't it be very costly?" I said. "I can't afford it. I want to pay for my share."

He smiled again in the convincing way of his. "Well, I can't afford it too often, but let me make up for not taking you to the beach. Next time, we'll talk about sharing."

A few days later, Lai told me that she was setting aside some money for me. I had never dreamt of asking her for money on top of all that I got from her. As my eyes teared up, she scolded me for being too soft.

Apart from that first time, we always went to down-to-earth places. Most often, we just went to Botanic Garden, with food packed from People's Park Centre.

*

When he asked me to marry him, I cried a bit. I reminded him of where I had been in my bad years. He told me that he wanted an honest woman and that he was not a believer in the idea of spoiled goods. We were in a hut in the Botanic Garden. There was another Chinese couple on a bench opposite us. We spoke softly, and so did they.

On the grassy slopes in front of us, there was a group of British families. Their children bounded all over the open space, the boys chasing a football, their parents joining them once in a while, even the mothers in their skirts, the girls playing a catch game. They had servants with them, women who looked like Lai, and they had an unending supply of sandwiches and bottled drinks.

The shadows were lengthening, and the mellow sunlight played on Tiong's face as he outlined his plans for a bigger business and a bigger role for himself. It was about a year since I had reached Lai's place on a muggy night, sweaty, exhausted, fearful. Now we stood in this magical place, with its scent of freshly cut grass and playing children. It would take us an hour to get back to our world, where there was smoke and sweat in the day and we were just exhausted enough to sleep at night. But at that moment, I felt I could hope. I could hope beyond my wildest dreams, hope for the best, and still be prepared for bad things.

Tiong moved towards me, and I stiffened. He opened his arms, showing me the scarred palm.

"Come and hold me. Give me a kiss," he said.

My forehead, cheeks and breasts tingled with a strange kind of warmth.

He sighed. "What?"

I stood up. The first contact with his body made me shudder. I felt faint. I grabbed his arm to steady myself. He put his arms around my shoulders without squeezing me. His chest pressed gently against my breasts. My head sank into the curve of his shoulder, and my eyes became wet. I did not cry much. He stroked my hair. I had left it loose, the way he liked it.

*

His friends, Guan Huat and Heng, were quite like him. They were confident and easy-going. Heng was married. His wife Lee Ping seemed a bit snobbish when I met her. We grew closer later. Our wedding was humble, of course, but Guan Huat and Heng dragged us to Wah Sang Studio on South Bridge Road for a wedding photo. Heng got Tiong to wear a coat and a tie. Lai surprised me with a gift beyond my dreams, a full-length light-blue cheongsam that I have preserved to this day. She scolded me when I cried as she helped me into it. In our photo, we look more confident than we felt then. In those days, we didn't smile for the camera. But both of us look quite pleased with life. I sit with my hands on my lap, my knees touching. Tiong has parked himself on a stool, so that he is higher than me. He has one hand on his thigh and the other on the back of the chair. Looking at him, you would never imagine that a few minutes before, he was complaining that Heng was choking him as he knotted the tie.

Tiong chased his friends away quite early on our wedding night. He used to share a room with the two of them. Lai insisted that he move in with us and pay her a rent of three dollars in return for getting a whole room for our use.

It was dark in the room. Through a chink in the window, the

din of Waterloo Street seeped inside. Tiong drew me to him, gently at first. Then he squeezed me harder. I hugged him back. That we could be physically close and want each other to be even closer, joined together, was something that I had never imagined possible. I shivered. He put his hand between my tiny breasts, and then, he ran it over them. I felt it pulsating with the thudding of my heart. I put my ear against his chest and listened to it throb.

He stepped back, and I heard his clothes rustle. He tugged at my tunic. I was slower than him, but soon his hands were caressing me, starting with my face and neck, quickly moving to the parts that interested him more. He did not push or grope or pinch or insert. My body pushed against his, and I gasped for air.

He pulled me down onto the mattress. His body covered mine, and I braced myself.

His breath slowed down. "I'm sorry," he said.

My tears were welling up again. "Is it because of me? Because I am spoiled?"

"No," he said. He kissed me on the forehead. He waited for my tongue to touch his. My heart beat harder, and my skin tingled all over as we kissed. He covered my hands and legs with his so that the weight bore down on me. "I want to sleep like this," he said.

I kissed him on the cheek. His warmth made me sweat. "You're crying again," he said. "You cry a lot." I moved my arm to wipe my eyes, but his fingers were there first.

Soon, I had to prod him in the side and tell him to get off me. I pressed my face against his chest, and he put his hand on my cheek.

I had got used to being woken up by the gradual stirring of life in the morning. From a distance, there would be the hum and honking of the first trolleybuses. Close to us, there were the bells of the Indian temple.

That morning, it was Tiong who shook me awake. Through bleary eyes, I saw that he was grinning. He covered my face with kisses. I stroked his head and told him I wanted to sleep some more. He took my hand and led it to his erection. He was panting, but he waited for me to open myself to him.

He looked into my eyes. His eyes shone, but it was a different light they had, different from all of my memories. In my bad years, I had mostly looked beyond the jerking animal forms of the men crushing me. It helped to pretend that it was not happening. Quite often, I had simply lain unconscious. The few times I had seen the eyes of those men, they had glittered with the delight of penetrating, of inflicting pain.

Tiong's eyes were half-closed and dreamy. He smiled and kissed me on either side of my mouth. Later I learnt that it was my dimples he was kissing. The pleasure of the act itself was all his, not mine. But I was content to give it to him. My arms held him tight. He moved gently, and he finished almost as soon as he started.

For the first time in my life, a man hugged me tight and kissed me after he had finished. I stroked his damp head. His heartbeat was erratic and loud. He hardened again inside me and started moving. He moved carefully, as if to make a point that he knew how to be gentle. He twined his fingers with mine as he thrust. Our bodies became slick with sweat. He bent down to kiss the point of my left breast.

He seemed to be losing steam. I told him that he had better stop. He couldn't do it twice so fast. He stopped pushing but stayed spread-eagled on me. I pushed him off and onto his back and lay down on him. His heart was still thudding.

"I'll go in a while to make coffee for everyone," I said. We had had coffee in the house for about a month by then.

He ran his fingers through my matted hair. He knelt and traced the scar on my right foot with his finger, gently. He did not ask about it. He sucked on my toe and made me shudder with pleasure. I pulled my leg away. We kissed again.

"I am spoiled goods, but I never kissed a man before," I said when we had finished.

"Stupid woman, crying again," he said. He picked up my tunic and wiped my face with it. "Go make coffee."

*

What is love? When Tiong held me tight after making love to me, knowing that a thousand men had taken me before, that was love.

10

Tiong's Story: On the Beach

1942, Lim Tiong

TIONG HAD BURNED so much that he felt icy cold. The scene had not changed much since he had squatted down many hours ago. There were rows and rows of heads of black hair packing the school compound. The heads were mostly very still. They drooped. The scene reminded him of a harvest ready for the scythe.

He had thought the sun could not climb higher. That it could not sandpaper the skin of his neck more than it already had. He was wrong. The heat became something physical, like a dog collar choking him.

He looked at the lines on his dirty right palm. The Kling who drove a bullock cart had told Tiong that with his lifeline, he would live till eighty. That thought had made the wheels of Tiong's mind whirr. Take all his life until then and triple it, and there would still be years left to live.

His cracked and mud-splattered toenails peeped out of the discoloured Bata sandals that his father's Ang Moh manager had gifted him. His knees were numb. The tail of his back hurt and urged him to stand up for just one instant. But he had seen what happened to the man who listened to that urge.

A month ago, his parents had prepared kueh. They knew it

would be the last time. The scents of all the things that went into it—especially gula melaka and coconut—had wafted through the house, each of them pleasant, but the whole of them so much more than the sum of the parts. His father's eyes were red. He told Tiong's sister she did not need to help with the vending.

Now, as Tiong sat in the sun, the mixture of smells of the compound took his mind off the murderous heat. The one smell that overrode all the others was of piss, borne from the corner chosen by the brave ones to relieve themselves. There was another smell, though, lurking in the background.

He had been a signaller at the Battle Box. It was a different time. The walls of regular stone blocks there had conveyed solidity. The Ang Mohs had the calm composure that came with superiority gifted at birth. Then the cracks had appeared, as the front lines shrank towards Singapore, as they crossed the strait. Tiong was not as frightened by the sinking of the two British ships as he was by the tremors in the voices of the officers. A smell of defeat had permeated the three-foot walls.

This smell bound his feet to the scorched ground. The Japanese sentries with their rifles were insignificant. The smell of defeat was the invisible web that tied all of them who squatted there. In his dreams, he often woke up sweating after struggling against a fishing net that wound itself tighter the more he struggled.

He could pretend this was a dream. Perhaps he should. A dream spiced with the senses of life. That thought freed him from heat, pain and thirst.

A flurry of movement brought all the sensation back. It had started in a distant corner, and it moved slowly. At its centre were three men. Two were impossibly erect, like toy soldiers. The one who seemed to pull them along walked in a shuffle. It took Tiong a while to understand what was special about him. Not his cowering posture. Nor his clothes—they could have been Tiong's. What was special was that he wore a black hood.

The three of them made their way to the centre of the compound, where Tiong was. At places, the man in the hood stopped. His finger pointed to one of the squatting men. One of the two smartly uniformed Japanese officers moved a finger as well. The moving fingers propelled the squatting man towards the side gate.

This had happened five times since Tiong started counting. Out of the many men sitting, few were chosen. The make-believe dream became silent as if someone had turned the volume knob all the way on a Murphy radio.

The man on Tiong's right had been insouciant all along. A short time ago, he had muttered a joke and chuckled to himself. Or perhaps it was a long time ago. Now he was wide-eyed and fixed his stony gaze on the ground. Was the pebble in front of him so interesting? He was shivering. If Tiong didn't have a lump in his throat, he would have told the man to imagine he was in a dream. Tiong looked hard at the other man for a long time—until he realized this was one of those times when someone whom you are looking at chooses to ignore you.

When Tiong looked up, three pairs of eyes were watching him. Two were framed by the rims of spectacles, one by the black cloth of the hood. The eyes of the man in the hood flickered as if they did not want to hold Tiong's gaze. They kept returning to him, though. If they could speak, they would have much to say.

Those eyes were familiar. The holes in the hood were bigger than they needed to be. The man's eyebrows were thick. They slanted upwards, and the one on the right had a scar through it. Tiong wanted to look away, but those eyes held his in a lock. Tiong gulped. His throat was dry and it hurt.

Those eyes lowered themselves. Their light dimmed. Tiong did not digest what happened for a few seconds. As those eyes turned away, the hand they were connected to rose. The most visible part of the man became the end of his finger. It pointed between Tiong's eyes.

Tiong's focus was drawn to the Japanese officer on his right. The officer gestured gracefully with his hand, making an upward movement. As Tiong rose, the strained muscles of his lower back and calves sighed with relief. The man who had joked—his neighbour—was looking at him now, his eyes were wide and moist, and he looked as if he had something to be sorry for. Then he closed his eyes.

There was a path for Tiong through the gaps in the ranks of squatters.

*

Something was wrong with the small of his back. A silent scream of pain started there. The scream drowned out the plaintive whispers of his calves and knees. The ground seemed to shift a bit, and the sky careened before steadying. The eyes of a dozen squatters were on him, urging him to move on, to remove himself and take the attention of the soldiers away.

When he walked, his feet did not seem to belong to him at first. This lasted for a few steps until the pins and needles attacked, and then a searing pain exploded in his ankles.

Others were ahead of him. He followed the blurs of their shapes. At irregular intervals, Japanese men in uniforms channelled the selected men along with tiny movements of their fingers, without a word.

He stepped into the gap of the gate and crossed it. His nostrils filled with dust and a smell of petrol that was almost pleasant as a truck rolled away, its rumble deafening for a few moments before it became distant.

Another truck inched forward and shuddered to a stop. It took a while for the remnants of the overpowering sounds of the two vehicles to fade into silence.

He stood there with two others first. Soon, their group swelled.

Four Japanese soldiers jumped down from the back of the truck with practised ease. Three of the four wore round glasses with black rims.

He was too close to the soldiers. He did not want to be the one facing them. But he could not shrink back. When he looked sideways, the men standing with him averted their eyes.

The only sounds now were shuffling footsteps behind him as more men joined them. Nothing much was happening. This is how dreams are, he said to himself. Sometimes time cascades, sometimes it freezes.

The squawk of a crow shattered the silence. The fluttering of its wings filled up the compound.

A grunt, a loud, "Hmm!" drew his attention. It was the one without glasses. He had a thin moustache. Like the rest of them, and unlike the first lot of Japanese soldiers they had seen at the start of the war, the man was shaved and wore spotless clothes. His second grunt had a higher pitch. He was short and muscular. He lowered his rifle a bit, and the mounted bayonet traced a path through the air. He had not spoken a word. He did not need to.

The truck was different from the British Bedfords. It was shorter and less imposing. It had a spare tyre mounted next to the driver's door. The plate at the back was lowered, and a ladder was in front of him. The empty cabin was bare and clean. It looked forbiddingly high. Tiong looked over his shoulder, hoping someone would step forward and climb up first. The man behind him was breathing heavily. His eyes were wide and frozen.

"Oooi!" A harsh cry jolted him. This time it was a guttural voice. Tiong placed his hands on the ladder. The first rung was too high. The backs of his knees and his shoulders hurt as he hoisted and pushed his weight up. His sweaty palms left wet marks on the ladder's bars. His right foot had developed a tremor, and his left foot seemed lifeless.

He crouched on the floor of the truck for a few moments before he willed himself to stand. His head swam again. There was light behind him, strong and warm, and darkness in front. He raised his hand to hold the metal truss on which the canvas cover rested. Involuntarily, his palm turned towards him. Glistening with sweat and streaked with mud and the rust of the ladder, it glowed against the dark. His lifeline stood out, bold, curved and unsullied.

*

The air behind him became denser. He looked over his shoulder. The man behind him had climbed the ladder. His breath was hoarse and shallow, as if he was about to burst into tears. He had lowered his head. Tiong could reach out to clasp the man's shoulder. Perhaps it would stop him from trembling. A shout from below, words that meant nothing but still conveyed meaning, interrupted the thought.

He moved forward into the darkness, to a corner of the truck's rear. The space behind was already full of sounds—the rasp of feet on steel, grunts and shouted commands. More men were clambering up. Soon, there would barely be space to stand. In the dark, he could see outlines of more of them. Men were now pressed against him. He felt the soft shoulder of one and the elbow of another. He smelled their sweat. In a different life, he had ridden a mosquito bus and pretended the other passengers did not exist. This time it was different. There was something different about the smell of them all. The fear in their hearts had seeped into their sweat. And his heart beat fainter, as if it was willing time to slow down.

His shoulder hurt now. He figured that he did not need to hold on to the grid above. The truck was not moving yet. It was a relief to lower his hand.

Almost right away, the floor shifted. He lurched on to his neighbours, and they rocked before pushing him back into place.

No one shouted at him.

The steady throbbing of the truck had turned into an angry roar. He raised his arm to cling on to the rod on the roof. His neighbours still did most of the work of keeping him in his place. He did not need to exert his shoulder too much.

He turned outward, away from the crowd. A reward waited for him. Fresh baked air ruffled his hair and brushed his cheeks. There was a jagged hole in the canvas just in front of him. He considered ripping it to make it bigger but could not bring himself to do it.

The hole showed a brightly lit world that had rejected them. The truck hurtled over a pothole, and the point between his balls hurt so much that the pain numbed it. He closed his eyes. When he opened them, he saw trees and attap houses. The Raja's house flitted by. Then the houses were fewer and further away. The air smelled of the sea. The scenery outside flowed in a stream of images as if it were a colour cinema, as if there could be such a thing.

*

The draught had dried him. His shirt felt starched. The vibrations of the truck's floor had calmed his tired joints. The truck had slowed down. It rocked as it traversed a muddy path between palm trees.

Something broke in the scenery. It took his exhausted mind a few moments to understand what had happened. The cinema had paused. He could see unripe mangoes on a tree not too far away. There was a loud roar behind them. Their truck had stopped for another one that was driving past in the opposite direction.

The floor jolted as the truck strained to get back on the road. The foliage started flowing across the frame of the hole in the canvas again. Suddenly, it became sparse and interspersed with patches of mud.

He had not looked at the men pressing in on him. He latched on to the outside view and never let go of it. Words were spoken, but he filtered them out. From somewhere behind, a man muttered in a gruff baritone. Whatever he was saying, Tiong did not wish to decipher it. Now those whispers increased in volume. The shrill hum of the insects became much louder as well. Another sound had faded away. The truck was gliding down a slope with its engine cut. When it finally halted, the stoppage was gentle. Almost immediately, there were thudding sounds of boots hitting the ground. There was a shout from the front, and the gibbering behind him stopped.

He did not want to turn back and face the rest of the men. He gazed at the sand, the coconut trees and the grey sea. Only when he saw the water did he hear its gentle slapping of the beach.

There was a clang as a bolt was drawn. The hatch at the back was opened, and the ladder lowered. The pressure from the men hemmed in on all sides eased a bit first. Then it disappeared as feet shuffled towards the ladder. The ride was over.

He wanted to keep his back to the crowd. He knew that he could not. As soon as he turned, he saw a man standing between him and the ladder. The man was bent and frozen, his eyes wide, and he seemed to implore Tiong to go first. Tiong stepped past him and patted his shoulder. The man was trembling.

The men below were busy. It was as if no one cared whether the two of them would ever climb down. The truck had stopped in a large gravel clearing rutted by other trucks like theirs. There were many of them there. A hundred, maybe two hundred. A few dozen Japanese soldiers fringed them. Two of them wore peaked caps.

There was a pattern to the activity. In a corner, soldiers were cutting lengths of telephone wire from a large unruly roll. One unwound the roll, and another cut it with a large pair of shears. A third soldier called the local men into groups of seven or eight and tied their hands together in jerky movements. The announcements had been in Chinese, and there were only Chinese men in the compound. Only now, standing on the edge between a past that had ejected Tiong and a future that he did not want, did this homogeneity strike him.

The shouts jarred. One officer was looking at him. From that distance, Tiong only saw the shimmer of the officer's round spectacles, but he sensed a fury in the eyes behind them. A soldier next to the officer raised his hands and gestured downwards.

Tiong did not need more persuasion. His hands and feet were steady as he swung his legs over onto the ladder. The other man followed. He was too close to Tiong. His breath was wheezy.

Tiong expected a shock when his feet contacted the ground. There was none. The mud was soft. A thought that he had kept bottled now oozed out. All of them here—what did the Japanese want with them? Did they plan to make them work, clean up the filth that had covered the city? But there was no work on Tanah Merah beach. And then, without a fuss, the answer announced itself. He knew why they had brought them here. He knew why the other man stood trembling, praying some miracle would freeze time. That man's cream shirt, crumpled and soiled now, must have marked him out as a prosperous man, perhaps an English speaker, when he reported to the school compound. That man, who was too stupid to dress plainly, understood where they were headed before Tiong did.

The heat was not oppressive now. The ride in the truck had cooled him, and the sun had mellowed. The man in the cream shirt and he were in the same group. Two soldiers approached, one of them carrying a roll of wire slung on his shoulder.

What would happen if Tiong ran? The thought buzzed in his mind, which found it too much of a burden. His feet felt heavier.

The group had lined up. The man in the cream shirt was ahead of him. No one spoke. One by one, they brought their wrists forward. His wrists were tied together, and he was tied to the man in front. He looked at his palm, bathed in the golden sunlight. The lifeline seemed etched in stone.

*

The Japanese soldier placed a black ribbon over his eyes. It had a defect, a tiny hole through which he could still see the world. The soldier's eyes were red, and his lips quivered. Tiong felt a gentle pressure where the telephone wire cut into his wrists. He followed the tug of the wire.

The man in the cream shirt staggered. His shoulders heaved with each step. Once, he turned his head all the way as if he could see Tiong through his blindfold. He made a formless sound. The wire jerked him forward. It tugged on Tiong's wrists as well.

On the beach, they had all slowed down. His feet sank deeper into the soft sand. The sand got between his soles and the sandals. If this had really been a dream, he would have kicked off the sandals and waded into the water.

Was it only last year that he was here with Shuheng? She noticed him looking at the curve of her ankle and smiled. She had let him hold her hand. A tingle had warmed all of him. He wanted to live to see her again.

They gathered in irregular groups, tied together. The wire had made marks on his wrists, but he did not feel hurt. Maybe this was a dream, after all. One didn't feel pain in dreams. He did not know who had ordered it, but they were being herded a little deeper into the water. The wires between them had been cut. Now the wire only bound his wrists.

The waves tugged at his feet, and the sun warmed the nape of his neck. A man in his group screamed. Tiong turned to him. His blindfold had come off. He was staring at a cement structure, with many holes in it, that straddled the beach. One of the holes was larger than the others. A long metal barrel poked out of it. The snout of the barrel traversed the length of the beach and then moved back.

The ground shifted below his soles, and his feet sank deeper. The gently massaging movement of the sand made him shiver. Someone to his left was moaning. He turned towards him, thinking he would tell him to shut up. But the noisy man's cheeks were streaked with tears. Tiong stayed quiet. A crow cried and landed on the top of the cement block. It fluttered away, leaving behind puffs of smoke.

The men to his right were falling into the water on their backs. They released dark-brown blots in the grey water. One man lurched and fell on him, bringing him down.

A great hurt exploded in his gut, where the falling man's elbow rammed into it. The waves turned silent. He could only hear a hard metallic banging. His ears filled up with water, and he was pinned down by two men. He was breathless. He pushed with his back, and one of the men on top of him slid away. He gulped big mouthfuls of air. The blindfold around his eyes was gone. The salt of the water stung his eyes.

The water around him was dark. The stink made him gag. On his left, a pair of boots was stepping on the bodies and the sand between them. A bayonet coated with muck descended at irregular intervals.

So this was not a dream after all. He knew he should lie still, but his chest heaved. He was crying. When they were very young, his sister and he had played here. She had made a mound of sand, and he had kicked it flat. He cried at what he had done. He wanted to be alive, in that moment from his history, and not do it.

The boots were now next to him. The tip of a boot scraped his left ear and numbed it. Then, the boots landed on his other side. The soldier grunted as his bayonet thrust downwards. Tiong's palm hurt as if a wasp had bitten it.

The pain jolted him. His eyes met the soldier's. The mellow sunlight played on the soldier's baby face. The soldier's eyebrows rose, and his eyes became misty. His shoulders sagged as he turned his gaze to the sea. He took a step sideways as a shouted command rang out.

Tiong closed his eyes. The murky brownish water had filled his ears. The man on top of him was very still. Tiong's eyelids were heavy. The sky had changed colour from blue to grey. It was a plain sheet without a single cloud adorning it. He wished he could float away. The last memory he had was of an agonizing, burning feeling in his right hand as the saltwater bit into it.

*

He woke up after what might have been a long and restful slumber. In his sleep, he had drifted but never left the sand. The sea had freed him from the weight of the man on top of him. He had an unfettered view of the sky. It had turned a dark grey.

His wrists were still tied. A piece of coral was poking his side. Perhaps it was this that had awoken him. He tried using the sharp edge of the coral to break free. He had to contort himself into various positions. It worked best when he held the coral between his knees and rubbed the wire against it.

He fell back into the sand as soon as he raised himself on his left hand. The beach was dotted with bodies. Some of them were floating in the sea. The waves were coming in deeper now.

When he stood, the world seemed shifty and uncertain. Was it his head or his eyes that made him dizzy? Or was it just the sand shifting below him?

As he walked away from the waves lapping at his feet, he navigated a passage with fewer bodies. He reached a cluster of trees to the left of the concrete pillbox. There was no one nearby. From a deep crevice of his mind, a memory surfaced—the receding rumbling of trucks as he lay on the beach.

He turned towards the sea. The half-moon was bright now, and the sand silvery. The beach had many men lying still. They could have been sleeping if it was not for their disarrayed limbs.

Then, some of them seemed to crawl. They were the ones deeper in the water. His knees hurt. He had fallen on them. He retched air. A scream was building up from his gut. He had no strength. A constriction in the chest stifled him. After a point, he gave up. His face was buried in the sand. He turned it sideways to be able to breathe.

*

"You will be fine," the Ang Moh doctor with green eyes told him. Tiong nodded. He waited, not knowing what to do. "You can go," the doctor said. He wore an army uniform, like the rest of the staff in the Field Hospital. Like them all, he had a haunted look.

Tiong bowed and walked out past the rows of men on stretchers. He was glad to be leaving. He had clear recollections of some points of how he got there but not of what happened between them. He was drinking water from a drain. This was after he left the beach. The water soothed his throat and made his belly hurt. He hid in a bush when he heard a gunshot and dogs barking far away. He spent a night in a pillbox and another in an empty house. He ate a raw mango, and his stomach hurt again. He was near Changi Prison when a group of haggard British soldiers talked to him. One of them peered at him and took him to an officer who wrote a note with a pencil and told him how to get to Raffles Institution. He said there were doctors there.

Now he walked past an arched doorway into the bright day. The sun was too bright, too hard. It hurt his eyes. He closed them for a moment. When he opened them, he could not help bringing his palms up. He stood there for a long time, looking at the place where his lifeline used to be. There was only a gash there now, dabbed with dark red Mercurochrome.

PART 3

11

On the Borderline

2005, Ah Ding

WHERE IS IT WRITTEN that we must flee death? There is an opening, a large window, at the end of the corridor. From the ground, the column of windows looks like a line of neatly punched holes, a bit like in a bus ticket, in the flat facade of the twenty-storey building. Standing at that window gives me a sense of space, of being in a different world.

I pushed that girl, Zhu Hua, away, naturally, but I wouldn't mind if she dropped in once in a while without asking me. She comes to the market once in a while, and without any drama, she buys a packet from me. She is nice, that girl. Nothing wrong with her. If she was here, I would talk about sleep, about not getting the little that I need. I wouldn't mention the images of my dreams—the hood suffocating me, a burning cheroot rammed into an arm, a finger bent backwards, a man tied to a ladder and being tipped into water.

How many nights is it now that I have longed for sleep but feared the pictures that it brings me? I have lost count. From a long time back comes a memory of being too cold to sleep, and too sleepy to get something to warm myself; a guardian angel taking me to a safe haven with a blanket. I have no one now, and now that the past has found me, when sleep takes pity and blankets me, those dreams yank the blanket off, leaving me panting. Why has all that come back to haunt me after so many years? It has to do with the woman who wants to help me, of course. But where was it written that we should meet again?

When I was a child—maybe five?—I used to play a game with my shadow. I would crouch, jump, run to shake it off. There was, of course, no getting away from it. I could spend hours playing that game. The shadow would become longer as the afternoon wore on. It would leave me only when all the ground became a shadow. The shadows gathered slowly at first, but they crept up and covered the ground in a few minutes at the end of the day.

All that we do to escape death is not too different from a child trying to jump off its shadow. The dreams that visit me now are dreams of 1942, the year I saved my life, at an age when there was so much to live for, even if it was not something I could describe clearly. I could explain what I did to myself then, as I can now. It was not only death I escaped but also pain. We are not all like that woman, the war heroine, what's-her-name, Elisabeth Choy. We are mostly people like me. It did not always take much pain to get people to do things back in 1942. They did not have to touch me. All they had to do was show me what they could do. I can explain it to myself, but it does not make the dreams go away now that my wounds have been reopened. The nameless woman is not the only one I helped. I saved many others. But the good I did does not cancel out the evil. If only I wasn't a fool, I would imagine that it does. If only.

Here, at this big window, there is a din in my ears. There are vibrations in the air that skims off the scents of the tall trees whose tops are just two levels below me. From behind me, the shrill sounds of the Tamil TV channel, *Vasantham* or something like that, waft out of the open door of the flat with the Indian family. They will not shut the door till eleven.

Beyond the trees is the main road, Lower Delta Road, and on the right, Jalan Bukit Merah. The bright street lights extend in neat, slightly curving lines to the horizon and beyond it. The traffic is still quite heavy. The red and purple buses are still running. There are more and more cars these days, with all the Chinese and Indians coming in. There is a lot of money in this city.

One of these roads must lead to her place, the home of the woman with whom I walked back in 1945 and who wants to help me now. The woman who has reopened buried memories because of which I stand here wondering if death can be such a bad thing.

Who could have known how much change there could be in the twenty-thirty years after the Japs surrendered? All these necklaces of bright lights, the hills with their slopes adorned with neatly trimmed grass, this garden city—this part of it has been built on a rubbish plain. Before that, long before, it was a beehoon plain where they dried beehoon. They broke down a hundred-and-twenty-year-old temple to build a swimming pool over it. Some kampungs that had to make way for the new flats like this one just happened to catch fire. Like at Bukit Ho Swee. With all the progress we have made, you cannot see the earth that this city stands on. You can see cement, grass, tar. Not much earth. This town where I live, everyone knows, is called Red Hill, and it became red when the Sultan ordered his soldiers to kill the boy who had saved the city from attacking swordfish because the Sultan thought the boy was too smart for his good.

There used to be a glass factory some distance on my left, on Henderson Road. There was Times House on Kim Seng Road, not too far on my right. All gone, all replaced with newer, shinier, glassier buildings. Great World City is now a mall. Just imagine.

In all this progress, some people did well for themselves. I escaped to Johor, and things got hot there, and when I came back, I lay low. The closest I came to a good life was when I drove a taxi. I gave it up after one ride in 1972, in which the passenger came close to recognizing me—or at least he sounded like it. That was the end of my taxi driving. There was a long stint in Queenstown Remand Prison, brought on by a small robbery, which became necessary to pay hospital bills.

When I think about it now, standing in the corridor, being fanned by the night breeze, I think life could have been better. But it could have been a lot worse in another place, like Johor. I am better off here, in my rental flat. I would probably be out on the street there.

How hard can it be to raise my leg over the railing, get my butt on the edge, and push myself off? I imagine it happening, and my breath quickens, and the part between my balls and my arse tenses up. Since sleep deserted me, my hands are weaker than they used to be. It will be hard to haul myself over. Maybe I could get drunk first. There's no cheap way to get really drunk, but that shouldn't matter. I peer over the railing. From here, I can make out the circular patterns on the cement floor below. I imagine the air that is caressing me now, turning into a howling wind, the hard floor hurtling up towards me. It makes me dizzy.

The texture of the light behind me changes. A fat woman has got out of the lift. She hobbles towards the other side of the corridor.

The moment has gone. I was here a couple of nights ago. I have stayed longer today. Maybe someday I will be here drunk, and that will be the day I will tip myself over across the finishing line.

Every square foot of this land below me is lit. The web of lights stretches as far as the eyes can see, and it makes my eyes heavy A familiar tiredness descends on me again. It is tiredness of the kind that smothers sleep. When I do linger on the boundary of sleep, I long for images of a girl who opens her arms to me in a scented forest on a moonlit night, but the images I get are of men I point at being told to move away with flicks of fingers. Of a man being hacked to death on another silvery night. Of the many ways men can hurt the men they have conquered. And the women, how they can hurt the women.

Those images have nothing to do with me, Ah Ding, the tissue seller who lives in rental flat #09–23. All those things that happened, those suppressed memories that have been smoked out, are of a different man, a man who might easily have followed a different path if he had started off from his house a few minutes later on the 18th of February 1942, or if he knew how to bow low enough to please a Japanese sentry. Or if he wasn't a bit of a fool.

That sinking feeling below my gut has left me. Is this as good a time as any to go over?

My eyes itch, and I give in to the itch. When I move my hands away, I know I have rubbed them too long. They are smarting. A ball of light appears before me. The shrillness of the hum of the crickets increases. The ball of light seems to contain a shape, a hint of a body. This is from a dream I have had before. The song of the insects and the noise of the traffic are snuffed out. There is only silence, and the thing in front of is morphing into a recognizable shape.

12

Grave Memories

2005, Siew Chin

IT IS QUITE A WALK from where Peter parked the car. It used to be a pleasant walk past the grave with the two dark, fierce Sikh soldiers. But today, it has been a bit much for me. My shirt is damp; my hands rest heavily on Michelle's shoulders on the way here. She has been eyeing me with increasing nervousness.

As we turn left to the two graves that I have come for, she tenses and pulls me to a stop.

"Look!" she says. I follow her pointed finger. A small wild boar scampers across the deserted track in the distance. Michelle is wide-eyed, like a child. "Did you see?"

"Yes, it's a good thing they are far away," I say. "I saw the baby."

"The mother was four times its size!" She lowers her voice to an awed whisper.

"Luckily, they are more scared of us than we are of them," I say.

At the tombs, she fumbles a bit as she places the folding chair on a small level patch in the grass. She makes it a point to hold the small of my back as I lower myself onto the canvas seat. I love the relief in my calves and the backs of my thighs as I settle down. I close my eyes, and the sounds of the cemetery fill my head. I decompose the many layers of sound—a bird making a rhythmic ululating sound, another one chirping at a much higher pitch, the hum of insects that is a mix of countless sounds. I already feel rested. I look over my shoulder. Michelle has stepped away, as she always does. Not that she would understand what I say, because if I did say anything, it would be in Hokkien. As it happens, I have nothing very much to say right now to Lai or to Tiong. I just needed to be with them.

Lai's tomb is more traditional and ornate, as it should be. Tiong took charge of getting it built. It has a tomb mound and a terrace. The oval tile that bears her picture has faded a bit, but it has borne the sun and rain of Singapore well over five decades. When Tiong died in 1972, Lee Ping and her husband did most of the work while I stayed in a trance for more than a week. I asked them to add a marble plaque to Lai's tomb, in English, similar to the one they had arranged for Tiong. The tombstones, of course, only have their names in traditional Chinese. Tiong's in golden letters on black stone, Lai's embossed in the cement.

It is two months since I came here. A creeper has flourished at the base of Lai's tombstone. The grass is a bit unkempt on Tiong's grave. We must get a round of maintenance done. My gnarled hands are folded in my lap. I realize my head is bent when my neck starts hurting. I raise my head, and the words start flowing in my mind. They don't change much.

The journey to this junction of place and time, me sitting here surrounded by this garden of tombs, was a long one, but most of it was mapped out many years ago. Was it really so long ago that we were in Wah Sang Studio, Tiong and I? The flash blinded me and made me a bit dizzy. I wanted to lean against Tiong, but it was out of the question. Just before the bulb flashed, I finished making out the letters on the camera, though I couldn't say them: "Brownie Reflex". And there I was, rolling a pineapple for luck in our new flat, squeaking, "Huat Ah!" I gripped the pineapple too hard, and its blisters bit into my palm. And then the phone was ringing. It was the call from General Hospital. If only Tiong had buried his own past ... What kind of monster was the man who pointed at Tiong? I push the thought away. As I always say, the days are slow, but the years go fast. And the decades, they just whizz by.

Now there's a straight and narrow path for me to dodder along until I stumble and stop. Lai and Tiong. I am lucky to have had two such people in my life. Together with the man with whom I went for that long walk, whose name I learnt only two months ago, they gave me a life that was beyond my imagination. The day I recognized that man, Ah Ding, and he recoiled from me, I saw the cardboard woman again. She was bent double, pushing a rickety cart stacked with flattened cartons. I would never sell myself, but I could easily have been her. I could have been dead. I could have been the one living in a rental flat. "The two of you," I say to Lai and Tiong, "made this life of mine possible. You both and that Ah Ding.

"How could you leave me so early that I only took from you and did not give back? Tiong, think about it, Lai was sixty when she passed away. In those days, in 1955, the year of the bus riots, life was unpredictable, sixty was an old age, and she left us after we had settled on the path to prosperity. But you, Tiong, you were fifty! And look how you blundered into death. All you had to do was talk, talk to me."

Michelle's hand is on my shoulder. I reach out to push it away, but on its own, my hand clings onto hers. She hastily pulls out a packet of Fairprice tissues. Her hands tremble as she wipes my cheeks. My tears are warm, and they irritate me. I did not come here to cry. Usually, I discuss plans and such like with the two of them, hear them out, and leave the cemetery feeling stronger.

I turn to Michelle to nod a thank you to her. I reach out again and take her hand in mine. Her eyes are moist.

"Let's go, Ma'am," she says.

I let her help me up and hold my hand as I walk over the uneven, grassy patch to the safety of the paved road. The path back to the parked car stretches out long and straight, bordered by damp grassy land covered with tombs. The thought of walking all that way exhausts me. I turn to Michelle for succour. She nods as if she has heard me thinking. She has the chair in her right hand. She lends me the crook of her left.

"You need a hot tea in the kopitiam cup," she says. "I'll make it superfast when we get home."

I try to walk a bit faster. My heels protest, and I give up. The light is fading fast. The clouds have lifted, and the evening has the same tint it did when Tiong proposed to me sixty years ago. The thought isn't enough to make me feel better. This is the first time in many, many years that I am leaving the cemetery unhappy. Maybe it is a sign that I should go soon.

"Don't say that, Ma'am," Michelle says.

"What did I say?" I ask.

She frowns and smiles at the same time. "I like coming here, Ma'am," she says. "I like what you said last time. When we drink water, we should think of the source."

*

All the soundproofing in the world can't filter out the roar of the sports car—I think it is the same one—that usually goes by on River Valley Road a bit after ten at night. Its ugly roar is not what woke me up. I have been gazing out of the floor-to-ceiling window, waiting for sleep to come to me, knowing it will be a long wait. I slept a bit too long in the afternoon before we went to the cemetery.

This pocketed-spring mattress cost four thousand dollars. As Lee Ping said, it is all right at our age. We won't take anything with us except a coin in our mouth to bribe the gatekeeper and the clothes we are shrouded in. I turn to the other side, which is a complicated procedure. I sleep with a pillow between my bony knees when I am on my side, which is most of the time.

Sleep is one of the many things money cannot buy. Leaving aside sleeping pills, of course, which I left aside years ago. The day has been heavy on me. I have lost interest in TV. Since *Holland V*, there has been nothing interesting. *The Champion* was ridiculous. It has been a long time since I went to Serene Centre to get a DVD. In the last six months, there has been a new problem. I can't hold books that are too heavy. It's strange to have to leave out books that are too thick the few times I go to the library. I go less often since they knocked down the old library to make way for a tunnel. Such is life, even when one has all the money one needs.

I raise myself slowly, pushing down with my left arm, and sit on the bed for a while. Through the tinted glass, beyond the scented, manicured garden, the headlights of the cars and buses are like dull dots. I could shift to the bedroom on the other side of the house, where the windows face the enormous swimming pool. But it is a long time since I overcame inertia.

What came over me in the cemetery today? I have been going there for half a century. For years, Tiong and I went to Lai's tomb. Later, I went alone. It was never a place of sadness.

My life would have been very different if it wasn't for my three saviours. That has been weighing on my mind, often, in the recent past. Perhaps it was that moment of recognition of Ah Ding that has brought on this latest round of disquiet in me.

I think of him sleeping on the floor, being grateful for a handed-down mattress, in his rental flat that would take me ten minutes for me to be driven to in my Bentley Arnage. I would need more time to get ready for the drive, but that's beside the point, as Tiong would say. I feel Tiong's eyes on me, gazing out in the dark from the photo frame.

I am wide awake now. It is no use pretending that I can go back to a tiring half-sleep. I get up and walk to the bell. The pain in my knees and lower back rises a notch higher, but I know that it will go as my body warms up.

When I turn the light on, it hurts my eyes first. By the time I have closed and opened my eyes, Michelle appears in her tight cotton T-shirt and tiny shorts. She has not slept yet.

"I want to go to the temple," I tell her. I expect her to make a face and issue one of her trademark exclamations: "Eh, Aiyoh, Hor."

She purses her lips and gives me that half-smile, half-frown again. "I call Peter to drive? Or we take a taxi?"

"What time is it?"

"Ten. You know the temple is closed, right, Ma'am?"

I place my hands on my hips. "I know it closes at six-thirty. But it's not a mall. We can still go."

She smiles more profusely. "I'll change in five minutes. I bring your dress?"

"No, I'll get it."

She calls the other companies first, unlike the rest of us, who always start with Comfort Taxi. She gets through faster that way. We get an SMRT taxi. There is a spring in her step as if she is excited by the idea of a late-night outing.

*

We stop at the Sri Krishnan temple first, as usual. It has been twenty years since they put an urn outside, and designated a corner inside for us, people who pray to Kwan Im, to pray there as well. The scent of smoke, sandalwood and jasmine rises from the joss sticks that have more or less all burned down since evening. I am glad I came at this time when there are only two tissue seller women in a corner. A woman who was here ahead of me is now on my right, bowing to Kwan Im, nodding her head in fervent prayer.

I like to take in the familiar, unchanging sights of the Hindu temple. The gate is flanked by two statues. On the left is a winged, crowned man, unusually fair for an Indian—but so are their movie stars—with his hands folded in a namaste. On the right is the

Hindu monkey god, their equivalent of Sun Wukong. I close my eyes and clasp my hands in prayer, and my mind flickers to my time in the cemetery and the unusual moodiness that descended on me there. I mouth the words "Om Mani Padme Hum". I open my eyes and run them past the colourful statues in the large panel above the gate. They look more arresting in the warm yellow light than they do by daylight. Or maybe the difference is that I have them to myself. A woman once told me the names of the boar and the lion avatars, but they were too complicated for me.

The Kwan Im temple is a few steps away. It is closed, of course, but this is also a good time to pray. I can see the statue of the eight-armed goddess in the dim light. I bow my head and recite the chant. Om Mani Padme Hum. I had no reason to believe in God in my bad years, and nothing that I saw since then has changed my mind. These two temples, with their tradition of cross-worship, have been a place to heal for much of my life. In a practical sense, it was the priests at the Kwan Im temple who protected Lai during the occupation. And of course, it was the landmark I trudged towards in these crowded streets on that fateful night in 1945. Still, both Tiong and Lai were much more ardent than me.

"I have come to pray for Ah Ding," I mumble. I am surprised at myself. This wasn't on my mind. "And for Lai and Tiong. I thank these two, who have changed body, and I ask for mercy for Ah Ding, who is still in this life."

A tingling starts in the middle of my eyes, spreads to the back of my head, rises to my crown and a bit higher.

13

The Gift of Lost Time

2005, Ah Ding

SHE HAS SUCKED UP all the light and sound that there was, and now I see only her and hear nothing. The air that was moist and warm, heavy and humid, laden with the smells of metal, concrete, burned fuel, bitumen, frying fish and a thousand other things, has turned cool and fragrant. It reminds me of another night. I think hard, but I cannot remember which one.

She has been looming in my dreams for many days now, this woman who is suspended in thin air before me. I saw the folds of her white robes, a large blurred lotus, a fuzzy human form that morphed between man and woman, growing hands and losing them—sometimes seeming to have a thousand pairs of hands. Today, in this dream, she has two hands. She has small but very visible breasts and fingers that seem too delicate to be of use in daily life. The lines of her face remain rather square and mannish, though her eyebrows are exquisitely feminine.

"Do you not know who I am, Ah Ding?" she says. I hear her, but I do not see her open her mouth.

"I know I am dreaming without sleeping," I say. In that silence, our words have faint echoes that mix with each other.

"But do you not know me?" she says.

"I see now," I say. "My time has come. That is good, it is fine. I was about to jump. But I thought I would see Yama in my dream. I am lucky to see you, Kwan Im."

"I have come because of who asked me to bless you," she says.

"I think I know who that is. But wait, it could be either that woman with no name or her niece Zhu Hua. I am lucky."

"She has a name," she says. "Though it does not matter now."

"No, it does not."

"Do you not want anything from me?"

"I do not know what to ask for anymore. I never prayed. I am sorry for that. I never believed."

"Do you not have a wish?"

"I wish I knew."

"You know."

"I want to erase those three bad years," I say. "The years I worked for them. Starting with my pointing to the men whom they killed, who I knew were going to be killed."

She is silent. Her face is impassive.

"Why did you ask me if what I wish is too much to ask?"

"It is too much to ask because it is not only about you. Those years were bad, and you were with those who made them bad, but there were many of you, and you yourself were less to blame. Still, they cannot be erased. Do you not wish for something for yourself and those you loved?"

"Is there such a thing as forgiveness? For what I did?"

"No."

"Then should I not just go?"

She smiles and vanishes.

Another woman appears. Even before she has taken form completely, she is reaching out. Her fingers, which I thought would be like cold marble, are soft, fleshy and warm as they wipe the tears away from my cheeks.

That is not the only surprising thing. The skin that her fingers touch, the skin of my cheeks, is not like bak kwa. It is soft and smooth.

It is Fusang. I am in a forest. Its sounds are deafening at first. The shrill part of the hum of the insects turns a tone louder as I take her hands in mine. She is still panting after running into the clearing. Her small breasts strain against her grey shirt that looks silvery in the moonlight.

She pulls a hand away to wipe the beads of sweat on her forehead and then takes my hands in hers again. I get it now that the scented night air I tried to recognize was of this night with Fusang. Her eyes are half-closed and moist. Her dimples show in the soft light as she smiles and raises her chin to bring her lips closer to mine.

When I do not step forward, she sighs, pulls her hands away and steps back. She moves with delicious slowness as her hands flit over the bottom of the neckline of her shirt and then move across diagonally. Her armpits show as she raises the shirt over her head, and then she stands bare-chested before me. Her nipples are taut and raised, jutting out of small aureoles that have tiny bumps.

All the scents and sounds of the world do not matter now. I hear her breath and mine. I smell her. She shivers as my breath touches her skin. A thin trickle of sweat runs down between her breasts.

"Kiss me first," she says.

I step forward, but she places a palm in my way. I fumble with my shirt, and my head gets stuck as I try to pull it over. She makes a tutting sound and eases it away. She lays our clothes neatly to make a covering over the grassy ground. She stands, tugs my hand and pulls us together. Her lips are soft but firm against mine. The first contact of our tongues and the softness of her breasts against my chest make me press her harder.

"Wait," she says, running her fingers through my hair. She lies down on the ground. I kneel beside her and look at every part of her. She touches my erection for just a second and giggles. The touch makes me shudder.

She blushes and goes down on all fours to let me look at her. Her buttocks and shoulder blades gleam in the moonlight. Then she lies on her back and opens her arms to me. I lie on top of her. She strokes the back of my head and presses down on it.

I hold the point of her left breast between my lips, suck on it, and then change to her right. She takes my hand and lays it on the other breast.

"I thought they would taste sweet," I say. "They are salty."

She is writhing now, raising her chest and pelvis in rhythmic motions. "You're still a fool, Ah Ding," she says with a smile. "Don't talk." She guides me with her hands. They tell me what to do, whether to be faster or slower, more insistent or less.

*

The end has been building up for a while as I move deeper and am unable to slow myself down. It starts with a pleasant warmth all over my body. The warmth comes and goes in waves of increasing intensity. In the end, the wave stays. I am burning and shivering. Our bodies are drenched in sweat. Fusang presses back against me, timing her thrusts to match mine. My back arches and I move deeper into her. I stay poised, and my body and spirit clench and unclench themselves until I finally collapse onto her, and my lips seek hers.

I do not know how much time has gone by. Our breaths are steady. She lies below me with her limbs open, sometimes convulsing and pushing up against me.

She runs her fingers through my wet hair and then over my face.

"Why are you crying?" she asks. "You'll always be a fool."

I nibble at her neck. "How about you?"

"I'm not crying now," she says. "I am a woman, and it was my first time."

"I should marry you, you should give me a baby, and I should drink your milk."

She laughs and kisses my head. She wipes my cheeks, and then, without warning, she starts sobbing. I hug her tighter. When her chest and shoulders stop heaving, she says, "We are lucky to have this. This is all we will get."

"I want to sleep," I say.

"Go to sleep."

I turn her over to her side and try to sleep with her breast in my mouth. I cannot breathe. She goes on her back and nudges me down so that my head rests on her belly. I lie on my side, loving the softness that rises and falls with her breath.

"Would it have tasted sweet?"

She pats me on the cheek. "Go to sleep. This is all we have."

I turn on my back and fold my hands on my chest. Her fingers gently caress my eyes. The night song of the forest fades out.

Epilogue

2005, Siew Chin

IN MY DREAM, Tiong and I are in the Queenstown flat and in bed, nudging each other to answer the doorbell. When I wake up, I am in a strange place. There is a figure leaning over me and shaking me gently. "Ma'am," she whispers. It is Michelle. She twists to draw the curtains. The light is blinding, even through the tinted glass. I usually sleep with the curtains drawn so that the room is lit by seven in the morning with sunlight. Michelle must have pulled them close sometime before morning to let me sleep longer. I wonder if she has slept at all.

"What time is it?" I ask.

"It's nine, Ma'am," she says. I expect her to laugh, but she looks grim. I stretch my arms carefully, downwards, before rising on my side. "The fixed-line was ringing. It was Zhu Hua."

"What is it?" I ask.

"She was crying. I told her you would call back from here." She hands me my mobile. I sit with my feet dangling. The screen looks blurred, but I can see enough to dig out Zhu Hua's contact and dial it. I already suspect what this is about.

Zhu Hua is done with crying. She tells me that she had the day off and went to Ah Ding's place after checking for him at the market. When she reached his flat, the door was open. She knocked and went inside when he did not reply. He was lying on his back, hands folded on his chest, completely at peace, dead. She called 995 and waited till they were there. On their way, they asked her to check if he was breathing, if his chest was moving. He was not. When they took a look, they told her it looked like a natural death in the man's sleep. They wouldn't tell her more.

"Are you okay now?" I ask.

"I think so," she says.

"Come over here. Have tea with me. I'd like you to be with me." I feel no shame as I say this.

"Do you want to go to the market?"

"No, I don't think so."

"Did I wake you up?"

"Yes, but it's very late. Take a cab. Don't … don't take too much time."

I end the call and try to straighten my back slowly.

In the bright light that bathes one half of the room, I look at the wrinkled palm of my right hand. I trace the long, curved lifeline with the nail of my left index finger.

Michelle is looking at me. I look back at her till I figure that she has just said something I did not register.

"What?" I ask.

"Shall I make the tea now? Hot milk tea in the kopitiam cups? With rice crackers?"

I look her over. Her eyes have dark circles. She probably woke up at the same time as every day.

"Will you have the tea as well?" I say.

She gives me that half-smile, half-frown.

"It's all right," I say. "I'll make it for all of us."

Glossary and Notes

Abang: Elder brother

Ang Moh: White people. Literally, "red-haired". Not intended to be pejorative.

Bak Kwa: salty-sweet dried meat (most often pork) jerky

Bak Kut Teh: Pork rib dish cooked in a herbal broth

Dalforce was a volunteer army formed by the local Chinese community to resist the Japanese invasion during the Battle of Singapore. One section, mainly communist, was directly led by Lieutenant Colonel John Dalley (after whom the army was named). Another section that was aligned to the Guomindang was led by Major Hu Tie Jun.

Gula Melaka: Palm sugar

Hokkien: Dialect spoken by a large number of Chinese in Singapore. Displaced by Mandarin and English after 1979.

Kopi: Coffee

Kopitiam: Coffee house

Kueh: Dessert, most often made with rice and by steaming

MPAJA: Malayan Peoples' Anti-Japanese Army, a communist guerrilla army.

Nasi Lemak: Rice cooked in coconut milk and Pandan leaves, served with side dishes such as anchovies, peanuts, sambal (a chilli sauce), and chicken or fish

Sook Ching was a purge carried out in 1942 by the Japanese military police in Singapore. Under this operation, Chinese males between the ages of 18 and 50 were summoned to screening centres. In some centres, hooded informants pointed out those Chinese men who had participated in anti-Japanese activities. Identified suspects were carried away in trucks and massacred. Tiong's story draws very heavily on a survivor's account (On *Changi Beach*, chapter in N.I. Low's *When Singapore Was Syonan-To*).

Teh: Tea

Wayang: Traditional shadow puppet theatre originating in Java. In colloquial use, used to imply that someone is putting on an act.

Bibliography and Related Reading

Geok Boi Lee (2005). *The Syonan Years: Singapore Under Japanese Rule 1942–1945*. Singapore: Epigram Books.

Gerard Sasges and Shi Wen Ng (2019). *Hard at Work: Life in Singapore*. Singapore: NUS Press.

James G. Farrell (1978). *The Singapore Grip*. London: Weidenfeld & Nicolson.

Jing Jing Lee (2019). *How We Disappeared*. London: Oneworld.

Ngiong Ing Low (1973). *When Singapore Was Syonan-To*. Singapore: Times Books International.

Noel Barber (1968). *Sinister Twilight*. London: Cassell.

Paul A. Kratoska (2018). *The Japanese Occupation of Malaya and Singapore, 1941-45: A Social and Economic History*. Singapore: NUS Press.

You Yenn Teo (2019). *This Is What Inequality Looks Like*. Singapore: Ethos Books.

Author's Note

I DEDICATE THIS BOOK TO MY PARENTS. After my parents, among those who have stood by me in my writing journey, I must thank Nolwen Henaff most of all, but also Archana Verma, Balwant Kaur, Mukul Deva, Meira Chand, Anand Raman, BA Krishna, Khalid Kureshi, my sister Meeta Kumar and my son Shreyas Kumar. In my writing group, I have benefited hugely from interactions with Xin Rong Chua, Nirmal Palaparthi, Louis Tong and Bjorn Klein. Sharmin Foo and William Chin provided detailed feedback on an earlier version of the manuscript. Yu-Mei Balasinghamchow's critique helped me to try to remove some major flaws in my work. I must thank the team at Balestier Press, of course, for giving me the opportunity to see this book in print.

The manuscript of *Lying Eyes* grew out of a course that Jing Jing Lee conducted at the Asia Creative Writing Program at Nanyang Technological University in early 2021. I did think that the course title, *How to Finish Your Novel*, was a bit over the top. I am grateful to Jing and my classmates for proving me wrong.

I thank the staff at the National Archives Singapore for their efficiency and helpfulness. I found a lot of useful information on the National Library's e-resources and on the blog Remember Singapore (https://remembersingapore.org/) and the "fellow nostalgia sites" that it points to. A 2019 lecture by Kevin Blackburn at the National Institute of Education, Nanyang Technological

University, gave me valuable insight.

Since I expect very few people will read my short stories, I have borrowed some lines from them in this work. I borrowed the names of two characters from a book by Yan Geling.

This is a fictional work. Characters such as the Chengs and Oishi in the story are not intended to represent the historical characters who had these names.